Puffin Books
Editor: Kaye Webb

THE VIADUCT

For over a century the Bensons, nearly all railway folk, had occupied the tall house close to the viaduct. Now only Phil Benson and his grandfather lived there.

Grandad was fond of reminiscing about the old Bensons, and sometimes mentioned Ebenezer Benson, the genius who had been a great engineer, yet had become a miser and died in obscurity. Phil wondered what had happened to his hidden money, and why he had never built his revolutionary locomotive. Had this anything to do with Jamie Benson, the boy who once carved his initials on the viaduct in 1843?

Phil soon guessed that Grandad told only part of the truth. What was in the attic? Why did Grandad make secretive visits there at night? Bit by bit, Phil and his new friend, Andy, set out to unravel the secrets surrounding the Benson past. But as they solved one problem, new mysteries arose which took them, again and again, to the viaduct, the Wasteland and the Cave. Others arrived in search of the lost fortune, and soon there were spies to outwit, and the ugly challenge of the Eccles gang.

Boys of ten and over will be fascinated by the authentic railway background to this story and the enthralling detective search to find the truth of what happened over a hundred years ago.

Cover design by Elisabeth Grant

Penguin Books

THE VIADUCT *by* Roy Brown

With drawings by James Hunt

Penguin Books Ltd, Harmondsworth,
Middlesex, England
Penguin Books Australia Ltd, Ringwood,
Victoria, Australia

First published by Abelard-Schuman, 1967
Published in Puffin Books 1969
Reprinted 1970
Copyright © Roy Brown, 1967

Made and printed in Great Britain by
Richard Clay (The Chaucer Press) Ltd
Bungay, Suffolk
Set in Linotype Plantin

Contents

Author's Note

Some of the places, happenings and people mentioned in this story are true. There is a district of south-east London called Deptford and the London and Greenwich Railway was a real company. A Colonel Landmann did construct the original viaduct, although there is no Deptford street named after him. In fact, everything Phil is told about the historical background of the viaduct is to be found in various history books.

There is also an area very like the Wasteland, with its footbridges, its junk heaps and a muddy path running alongside the arches, many of which are used in the ways described. But there is neither an Eccles Yard nor an Arum Street in Deptford. The long garden, and the 'jungle', are also inventions, and though it is true that engine workshops once existed somewhere beneath the arches, the ones referred to here are not intended to represent them.

As everyone knows, George Stephenson and Richard Trevithick were real pioneers, but the Bensons are imaginary people and I doubt very much if there was ever an Ebenezer Benson who designed a locomotive called *Stormrider*.

1 The mystery in the attic

The Benson house, in Deptford, stood apart from its smaller neighbours on the corner of Landmann Street, a stone's throw from the railway. It was a high, narrow dwelling with a frontage as flat as a disdainful face. Its tall windows had broken sashes and smeary panes – collectors of shadows and smuts, admitting both daylight and air as unwelcome intruders.

The viaduct bearing the railway passed slantwise at the foot of the street. The trains clanked and trundled so close that for George Benson and his grandson, Phil, it was like living in a railway station. They could practically tell the time by the different vibration patterns of the trains. One would rattle the cups and saucers in the dresser, but not the plates. Another set heavier dishes chattering like giants' teeth, the teapot lid clicking nervously in unison; and there was a train of cement wagons, hauled by a monster diesel, which had the peculiar effect of sending the living-room table throbbing several inches across the linoleum.

Phil and Grandad lived upstairs. Years ago, when Phil's parents were newly married, Grandad let them make their home on the ground floor. It would, he said, twinkling, be more convenient for prams. In time to come Grandad scraped together enough funds to provide an extra kitchen and a bathroom so that he could remain independent and 'not be a nuisance'. Bensons, he was fond of saying, had lived in this house for a century and a quarter. When he was gone, he wanted his younger son Alfred, who was Phil's father, to carry on the tradition.

But tragedy ruined the plan. Before Phil was five years

old both his parents were dead. Strangers came to lodge downstairs and Phil moved up with Grandad.

Grandad doted on Phil, and he did his best to provide him with all he needed. This was not an easy task for an old man. His ideas were a little old-fashioned and sometimes he made mistakes. There were plenty of critics who looked disapprovingly at Phil's quaint clothing, or said that the child was undernourished and sickly. They didn't realize that the hunched, pale appearance was merely a family trait, and that beneath, Phil was as robust and wiry as most of the tough youngsters who roamed the Deptford back streets.

When people hinted that the task was beyond him, Grandad took it hard and brooded. Once he said, 'Maybe them nosy parkers are right, boy. I ain't cut out to be a mother. There's things you're missing, things a young 'un's entitled to.'

'What things?' asked Phil.

'Well, things like being tucked up in bed at night, an' fairy stories, an' proper food . . .'

'I do have proper food.'

10

'Ah, but it's mostly out of tins. An' it's not only that . . .'
Grandad thought of farms and trees and sunshine, and his
dreams for Phil grew golden, unreal but compelling. 'You
could go and live with foster parents, like they talk about
down at the Welfare Office. Plenty of people would be glad
to take on a bright little lad like you. They might turn out
to be grand folk with pots of money. Then you'd have
holidays in France, an' rides on a pony, an' maybe an
electric train set. You'd go to a posh school an' wear one
of them smart blazers with a gold badge on the pocket. . . .'

Phil wondered, for an unhappy moment, if Grandad
were trying to get rid of him. But he quickly sensed that
the old man was only trying to do what was right. He said,
solemnly, 'I want to stay here with you, Grandad.'

Grandad breathed more freely. 'Ah, well . . . in that
case let the nosy parkers jaw their heads off. We'll show
'em, won't we, boy?'

There were other problems in the early days – those
lodgers downstairs, for instance. They were a shifty, fly-by-
night breed, who either stayed too long and gave the house
a bad name, or departed suddenly, owing the rent. Grandad, who was so canny and cagey in some ways, tended to
be too easy-going with his tenants. Eventually, a kindly
Welfare Officer discovered Mrs Partridge, the middle-aged
widow of a railway guard. In exchange for cheap accom-
modation, she would keep an eye on Grandad and Phil,
cooking, cleaning, and confounding the gossips. They
were soon devoted to Mrs Partridge and she to them. It
helped, somehow, that they were all railway folk. Nearly
all the Bensons, way back, had been servants of the railways.

As he grew older, Phil rarely thought of his parents,
whom he scarcely remembered. His father had died in a
shunting accident. His mother had succumbed to a serious
illness a year later. Their snapshots were on the mantel-

piece of their living-room, which was at the front of the house facing the viaduct.

The rooms seemed full of photographs. More snapshots pictured comparatively recent occasions; aunts, uncles and cousins smiling on seaside beaches or promenades, or in haphazardly arranged groups in back gardens. Phil remembered none of these people in the flesh, although Grandad said that a few of them had made occasional visits to the house and had attended the funerals of Phil's parents.

Only one name stuck in Phil's mind – that of a short, sullen man who glowered from a deck-chair against a sea wall at Southend. His countenance, Phil guessed, was only preserved because the snapshot included other members of the family. Occasionally Grandad referred to him in terms of bitterness and disapproval: 'That's your Uncle Ernest, boy. We don't have nothing to do with him, nor his flighty wife, your Aunt Luce. They used to live around here, but that was years ago.'

Phil gathered that Uncle Ernest, Grandad's elder son, had been a great disappointment and had left the district in some sort of disgrace. Not least of his shortcomings, apparently, was that he had been 'too idle' ever to have sought a job on the railways, as all self-respecting Bensons should. He was a 'ne'er-do-well' and a 'trouble maker'.

But most of Grandad's talk was reserved for a second group of photographs – the framed portraits of an earlier generation of Bensons which hung on cords from the picture rails. These were stiffly, formally posed. The clothes were dark and heavy, and many of the figures wore railway uniforms and carried the equipment of their trade with the pride of dragoons bearing arms. The faces of the male Bensons were bearded, or mournfully moustachioed; faces stern, faces staring . . . had the older Bensons never smiled? And Benson children. 'That's me, boy – the perky young lad in a sailor suit' – standing bewildered and overdressed in front of enormous family assemblies.

Names accompanied the prodding of Grandad's forefinger: 'That's Timothy. Now, he was *my* grandpa, Phil. Used to be a bobby on the old South Eastern. They used to call signalmen bobbies in them days. . . .'

Often a remark of this sort would set Grandad yarning throughout a winter's evening. He would begin by telling Phil some old story, and Phil would listen for a time. Then it all became too complicated to follow; and in any case Grandad, once his pipe and his memories got going in harness, would tend to forget that Phil existed. There were so many Bensons that Phil couldn't even begin to sort them out. And what was more confusing still, sometimes Grandad's reminiscences delved beyond even the oldest of the baffling array of portraits. There had, Phil realized with amazement, been Bensons who had lived, and died, too soon for their faces to be represented in those framed pictures. They, too had names. But it was even more difficult to remember, and sort out, names that had no faces.

There was, however, just one name that Phil remembered, not because it had a face to go with it but because, for some unfathomable reason, it always made the little Phil giggle. Ebenezer . . .

'Ebenezer Benson, the engineer,' said Grandad. 'One day I'll tell you more about him. Now you shouldn't laugh, boy – 'tain't respectful! He was one of your ancestors, the one who built this house, not long after the viaduct was done. He was a bit of a genius. . . .'

Phil was not sure what a genius was.

'All that is going back some, of course,' remarked Grandad.

Phil nodded, his face serious, now, and his eyes bright. It certainly *was* 'going back some'. It was history, and perhaps they didn't have cameras in history, so Ebenezer did not have a face on the wall. On the other hand, there was a picture of the viaduct, as it had looked in history. But as Grandad explained, that was a print from a drawing, not a photograph. It hung in Phil's bedroom.

The print was delicately tinted and it showed a long stretch of the London to Greenwich railway as it had looked when it was the first railway in the capital. The viaduct ran with a graceful loop of its arches across a green countryside with London's older buildings lightly sketched in the background. Above, a pale blue sky held no cloud. Leafy elms rose above the parapet of the railway where a squat, tall-funnelled locomotive shed a feather of white smoke. Attached to it was a family of three squat, gaily coloured coaches.

Often Phil fell asleep with the print in his mind's eye, and during the first drowsiness the impression would slip into half-dream. It was not that the scene sprang to life, yet something living was added to its sterile over-perfectness. In Phil's imagination a bird settled on the parapet and folded its wings, or perhaps a horse and carriage would canter surprisingly into the picture, or the elm leaves shiver as though wakened by a wind.

But in the morning the real viaduct, no longer elegant, cast its long, flat shadow across the streets. The squeal of engine brakes and the wail of whistles were like cock crows.

So there was the old Benson house, and the photographs of Bensons past and present, and Grandad's yarns, and that mysteriously real picture of the viaduct. And, as if all these were insufficient to set an imaginative boy's mind wondering and thinking, there was also Grandad's dwarf, Cobber McCoy.

Until Phil was seven or so, Cobber was at least as real as Santa Claus. Cobber McCoy was born because of the damp. Whenever it rained heavily, moisture seeped through the walls of the house, then dried, leaving patches of wallpaper brown and peeling like the skins of onions. And the same thing happened on the ceiling of the living-room, too, except that up there the stain was the size of a man's hand, directly above Grandad's easy chair.

Grandad would chuckle knowingly: 'There goes Cobber McCoy again, upsetting his grog.'

Long ago, Grandad had explained: 'He's a sort of hermit man, an' he ain't got nowhere else to go, so we lets him live in our attic – him an' his old cat, Toby. Only we don't disturb them, see, boy, on account of Cobber being nigh on a hundred, an' tetchy, an' that cat of his has claws like needles.'

Phil's eyes would widen with belief and fright. Up there, by candlelight, the shrunken, dwarfish figure lived out his days, never seen but much imagined. He had huge, pointed ears, a face wrinkled like tree bark and a wary, glittering stare. And the cat, Toby, a creature of nightmares, with saucer-huge eyes and a back arched like a grotesque, black caterpillar. Sometimes Phil lay in bed and, in the silences between the throb of train wheels, would hear the hiss and bubble of the grog brewing above the ceiling.

Then, at last, Phil had his very first glimpse into the attic. One night he awoke, sharply aware that some unusual sound had broken into his sleep. He sat up, saw that the tall rectangle of curtain was blank and dark, but there was a sliver of pale light under his door. The sounds outside were repeated ... scufflings, scrapings. He got out of bed, carefully turned the handle and peered out on to the landing.

A set of wooden steps stood astride the space between the rooms. A second strip of light shone through the partially open living-room door next to Phil's. Above,

The Viaduct

Grandad was almost at the top of the steps swishing a torch into black emptiness. The attic hatch over the landing had been removed, and Phil saw into the yawning cavity: a slope of thick, dusty rafters and boxes and bundles swathed in shadow....

Suddenly Grandad sensed Phil's presence. He half turned, teetered dangerously on the steps, then shone the

torch down into Phil's face. His chuckle came after a startled hesitation, and it did not ring true – neither did the explanation that followed: 'Just taking old Cobber his supper, boy. Better get into bed, or you'll catch cold.'

Phil obeyed. But he lay awake for a while, listening. He heard soft, weak thumps like bony knees crawling. The old man's night-cough floated in the hollow head of the house. And before Phil fell asleep again he was sure that such night disturbances had taken place before. On earlier occasions he had been too sleepy, or too incurious, to investigate. Now, what he had seen brought such hazy memories into sharper focus, and he knew that Grandad had made other visits to the attic at night, in secret.

There was something else: Grandad had fibbed. He'd been carrying no food – nothing save his torch. Besides, Grandad should have known by now that Phil was ceasing to believe in Cobber McCoy. The obstinate pretence, and the untruth, must mean that Grandad had a secret – a big secret.

Phil could not bring himself to ask Grandad outright what lay in the attic, nor why he went up there. Grandad did not mention the incident, nor did he ever again make jokes about the damp patch on the ceiling. Cobber and Toby were dead. So, for a time, was a small part of Phil's bond with Grandad. Of course, secrets were like that; if there were no sharing, something in a friendship withered. Grandad had put a wall between Phil and whatever was important about the attic.

'Perhaps,' said Mrs Partridge, 'he's only worried about the leak in the roof.'

'Then why not say so?'

This was some weeks after the incident on the landing. Phil could talk to Mrs Partridge, even about secrets, and know she would not betray him, nor gossip to others. Now, downstairs in her kitchen, with Grandad out walking, she got on with her cake mix and did not encourage Phil too far.

'What steps are you talking about?'

'Oh, just some old steps we keep up in our kitchenette.'

'I hope they're safe!'

Phil gave her kindly, rather puddeny features a sideways look as she bent over the table. His own face was pale and intent, his shoulders hunched from keeping his hands in his pockets.

'D'you reckon ... there's something ... hidden away up there?'

She smiled, her eyes suddenly flashing like a younger person's. 'People who ask questions like that usually have their own answers ready. What do *you* think?'

'At first I thought perhaps he'd lost something. But in that case, why not ask us to help him look? Why get up in the middle of the night and snoop about on his own?'

'It probably wasn't as late as you thought. Did you look at your clock?' Phil shook his head. 'Well, there you are. And in any case, elderly people often have trouble with sleeping.'

Phil shrugged. 'I think he's got something hidden up there – something he doesn't want me to know about. That's why, when I was smaller, he told that yarn about Cobber McCoy. And I believed!'

Mrs Partridge smiled at Phil's self-disgust. 'All elderly folk have their secrets, Phil. Your grandad's lived in this house all his life – that's seventy long years. In that time he'll have collected a lot of treasures. . . .'

'Treasures!'

'Now, don't let your imagination run away with you. They're not likely to be valuable, except to your grandad. Just relics, little heirlooms ... things a lonely old man likes to brood over. The Bensons, since way back, have always been simple, railway folk.'

'What about Ebenezer the genius?'

Mrs Partridge's hands stopped moving for a moment. 'Oh, that old tale! Your grandad thinks he was the eighth wonder of the world, doesn't he? But bless his heart, you have to take what he says with a pinch of salt.'

'So he has told you about him?'

'Not much. Your grandad doesn't talk a great deal about his private affairs, but I think he has a bee in his bonnet about the old Bensons. Still, it's none of my business.'

She put the cake in the oven, then poured a glass of milk for Phil. 'And it's none of yours, young man, until your grandad chooses to tell you. Now mind, no peeping into that attic when nobody's looking!'

'Of course not!' said Phil, blushing. Borrowing those steps trying to reach the hatch and taking a look beyond . . . that's just what he had been trying to buck up courage to do.

But perhaps Mrs Partridge was right, and there would be nothing of interest to see, Phil tried to remember exactly what he *had* seen during that brief glimpse by torchlight. Just a few ordinary boxes, shapeless bundles . . . nothing else.

2 The names on the tomb

Mrs Partridge's warning had its effect. Phil felt ashamed
that he'd ever considered opening the attic hatch for himself, and for a long time did not give Grandad's secret
much thought. When, as occasionally happened, he awoke
at night and was aware of movements on the landing, he
merely shut out the sounds by pulling the sheets over his
head and going back to sleep.

Mostly, Grandad and Phil spent the evenings snug and
contented with each other's company. Sometimes they
listened to the radio, or went downstairs to share Mrs
Partridge's television. They played ludo and snakes-and-
ladders, or arranged Phil's clockwork train set on the table
and made tunnels and bridges out of cardboard boxes.

But often, when twilight deepened quickly over the
streets, they didn't bother to switch on the light. Grandad's
pipe glowed red in the corner beside the fire, and he would
delve into his memories, thinking aloud, his voice a mono-
tone as soothing as a river's flow. Names, happenings. . . .

'I've told you about my old granny, haven't I, boy,
Maggie Benson? She was Timothy's wife. She were a real
tartar, but she could sing like a canary – used to 'company
herself on the piano. They had a piano, those days, down
in the parlour. An' big old ovens where Maggie baked the
bread. I can taste that bread now, boy – still warm, an'
buttered thick. Old Timothy, he finished up station master
down at Greenwich.'

Whenever Grandad mentioned the successful Bensons
there was pride in his voice, but something else, too. Phil
eventually realized that it was envy, because Grandad's
own job with the railway company had been comparatively

humble. For most of his working days he had driven a horse and van about the London streets between the termini, delivering parcels and crates.

Once Grandad said, 'It were a proper dead-end job, boy. You're going to do better. We'll make an engineer out of you, but engineers need a lot of book learning these days. I want you to pay attention to your books.'

It was the winter of Phil's tenth birthday. He had always done well at school, but suddenly Grandad, normally so easy-going and not in the least strict, demanded that he do better still. He even went to the trouble of borrowing thick, unsuitable textbooks from the public library, and dog-eared copies of the classics, and made Phil read them and work at exercises in English grammar and mathematics.

It was not long before Phil made a new and puzzling discovery. The old man corrected his sums readily enough, but when Phil stumbled over the long words in his difficult 'readers' he was bewilderingly unhelpful. One night Phil, tired and frustrated, blurted out his sudden, dreadful suspicion. 'Grandad, I don't believe *you* can read – can you?'

Phil never forgot how Grandad's face turned to ashes. 'What d'you mean, you young scamp? Of course I can read.'

'Well, go on then – show me!'

Grandad picked up the book and flung it aside. 'If it's too hard for you, why don't you up and say so, instead of making excuses? You'd better get on with your sums.'

Phil hated himself for what he had done. He had not meant to be cruel. It was just that he'd always assumed that all grown-ups could read. It was easy, now, for him to remember that Grandad never read a book for his own pleasure, and only glanced through the daily newspaper. Phil was quite unprepared for the hurt and humiliation the old man felt when his defect was discovered. Nor did he realize that it was possible to be quick-witted, yet word-blind. A few people – intelligent people – needed exceptional patience and care in order to overcome this weakness. Grandad's schooling, early in the century, had been scanty, and the teachers of those days had been too impatient and overworked to give him much attention. No doubt they had made poor George Benson stand in corners and regarded him as a duffer. This had hurt ever since.

Grandad kept up the pretence for a time. Cunningly, he made Phil read passages from the Bible – passages which Grandad knew by heart: many of the psalms, parts of St John's gospel and the Book of Proverbs. Now he *could* put Phil right when he hesitated, and Phil was almost deceived. But one day Grandad grinned, ruffled Phil's hair and chuckled, 'Maybe I'm not much of a scholar, boy, though I'm all right at figuring. But you'll be different. You've got the head, and we'll make you into a great engineer like your ancestor, Ebenezer.'

Phil jumped when he heard the name. It had been so long since Grandad had mentioned him. 'Grandad, what exactly is a genius?'

Grandad looked back over his pipe and the pride shone out of his eyes. 'There ain't one of them in a million, boy. But that's what Ebenezer was. You've heard me talk about Timothy, the station master who was my grandpa? Well, Ebenezer was *his* dad. And he designed engines. He ought to be in the history books, along with George Stephenson and Richard Trevithick. Before he come south to Deptford an' built this house, know where he worked? Up in Newcastle, with George Stephenson. You'll have heard about him at school.'

Phil nodded. 'Why isn't he? In the history books, I mean.'

Grandad took time to relight his pipe, then he waited for a train to thunder by on the viaduct. 'There are

reasons. . . . He was a pretty rum character, was Ebenezer.
Things went wrong for him, that's all.'

'What things, Grandad?'

'Nobody knows the rights of it. He was a hot-headed
character, so they say, an' he fell out with George Stephenson, an' that's why he come south. . . .'

'When you said, "they say", who did you mean?'

Grandad thought over his answer, fingering his white
moustache. 'Well, my old dad, Nathaniel, mostly. He was
a great talker – even more so'n me!' He seemed to make
up his mind about something important. 'You keep on
with your lessons, an' maybe some day I'll show you something special. You're getting to be a sharp lad, an' there
are other things you should know.'

Later, Phil was sure that this promise had to do with whatever lay hidden in the attic. But he may have been wrong.
Perhaps Grandad had been only thinking of the visit they
were to make to the churchyard.

The following Sunday, the second in November, Grandad cooked the breakfast as he always did on Sundays to
avoid disturbing Mrs Partridge too early. After the meal
he announced, to Phil's surprise, that they were going to
church. Phil attended a Sunday School regularly, but
nowadays Grandad's religious devotions rarely got beyond
good intentions.

Grandad dressed in his threadbare Sunday suit, waxed
the ends of his moustache, let Phil help him on with his
great-coat then took his silver-headed cane from the little
recess in the kitchenette where the brooms and step-ladder
were kept.

The day was raw but clear. The pavements were wet
after a night's rain – black mirrors shimmering with scurrying feet. There wasn't much traffic about, but Grandad
kept a tight hold on Phil's arm as they crossed by the

telephone kiosk near the house. Soon they were heading for the long, cluttered path that followed the viaduct into the centre of Deptford.

This was where Grandad walked nearly every day on his 'constitutional', sometimes going into the shopping centre for his tobacco, or taking a stroll along the bank of the canal. Phil, who had accompanied Grandad here before, knew there would be a history lesson.

Grandad pointed with his stick up at the viaduct parapet. 'That's where the first trains in London passed, boy. Folks paid sixpence and got from London Bridge to Greenwich in twelve minutes. *Twelve* minutes – an' they don't do it much quicker'n that now. This path used to be a boulevard, with trees, like you can see in that print in your bedroom. It cost a penny to walk on it. On Sundays, they say, people could stroll along the railway itself – ladies and gents in their Sabbath finery – because the trains only ran week-days. An' the nights ... well, it was a pretty sight on account of the gas lamps strung all along the parapets. They was like gold necklaces – that's what my old granny used to say, and she saw them when she was a child. . . .'

Grandad paused beneath an arch to get his pipe going. A rare Sunday train thundered over their heads. Then they strolled on, the chill wind whispering in the archways. Farther along, he tapped a door with his stick and said, 'There used to be stables here, an' Maisie was born not far from this spot – did I tell you?'

Yes, Grandad had told him, but Phil shook his head tactfully. Maisie had been Grandad's favourite mare on his delivery round.

'I bet the trains used to frighten the horses,' said Phil.

'Not Maisie,' chuckled Grandad. 'Trains ran in her blood – like they do in us Bensons!'

Most of the arches were closed in, used as storerooms and workshops. The frontages towered like the entrances to cathedrals. Some were of corrugated iron, others of timber or bricks. Most had man-height inset doors, heavily padlocked and secured with lengths of rusty chain. Mysterious numbers in white or yellow paint were daubed on their faces. Phil wondered at the great variety of things to be found inside. Even on Sundays, work was carried on and there were comings and going of trucks and motor cars and delapidated vans. Odd, varied sounds came from the arch interiors: a hammer's tinkle, the hum of generators, the plaintive scream of a sawmill. Once, voices in a foreign tongue came eerily out of a high ventilator grille. There were many different smells: wines, oils, vinegar, chemicals ...

Over a second footbridge, then a third, with a swift view of the canal wharfs where one fat, stumpy crane wrestled with heaps of timber. High and crowded together, shortening the horizon, towered flats and tenements with flat roofs festooned with washing lines. Children's voices screeched and their quick, eager feet clattered in hollow stairwells. Smoke beat down, bringing ash-specks mingled with sparrows' feathers and flecks of waste paper.

Grandad was still talking about the viaduct. 'Built by a bridge and canal engineer, name of Landmann – a colonel who served with Wellington, my old dad told me. That's how our street got its name. They changed it as a sort of tribute ... everything's changed, boy. Well, maybe not everything. Not the viaduct, not really ... not since I was a lad. I used to play over here before I was your age. Come to that, all the Bensons trod this path, all the way back to Ebenezer himself. Think of that, boy, that's history, ain't it?'

They emerged at last out of a tangle of half-demolished terraces, and walked along the High Street till they reached the iron gates of the churchyard, then on to the church.

And after the service, Grandad took Phil to visit the Benson tomb. Phil remembered the angel from a much earlier visit. He stood taller than a man, one arm bearing a sculptured scroll, the other raised in a benediction, or a beckoning. His face, chipped and worn by the passage of time, was still strong, wise and serene.

The grave was enclosed by a flat, stone slab overgrown with ivy dripping wet from the rain. At one end stood the angel and at the other a vertical stone, blackened with age, on which the roll of names had been carved. The names were of slightly different sizes and styles, crowded tight together and, in some cases, barely legible. Grandad intoned them all, slowly but with confidence – he knew them by heart:

> Here lieth Jamie Benson
> Beloved son of Sarah and Ebenezer
> Who died aged 11 years
> May 12 1844
> Likewise Ebenezer Benson, Engineer
> 1805 – 1846

Then followed the others: Stephen Benson, who had lived from 1770 till 1851; Sarah, wife of Ebenezer; Elizabeth their daughter who had not been laid to rest until 1884. There were Grandad's grandparents – Timothy, and his wife Margaret.

Grandad parted the ivy with his stick so that Phil could see the last of the inscriptions, but Phil's eyes were fixed thoughtfully on the first name – Jamie Benson. He was suddenly quite sure that Grandad had never mentioned him. Why not, since he was the first to be buried here, and had died so young?

Phil did some mental arithmetic. 'Did Ebenezer buy the angel for Jamie?'

'Could be.' Grandad was watching him reflectively. 'It's what they calls a family grave. Ebenezer might have bought it for Jamie in the first place, though.'

'Who was Stephen?'

'Ebenezer's dad. He come down from Newcastle with Ebenezer and Sarah – an' the young 'uns.'

'Elizabeth was Jamie's sister, and Timothy's?'

'You've got it.'

'All the Bensons aren't buried here.'

' 'Tain't that deep! These are only the Newcastle Bensons, 'cept for Maggie. Your grandma, an' all the rest of us, are buried in other places, or still living. For one reason and another the grave was closed for keeps at the end of the last century.'

'Tell me more about Ebenezer, Grandad – and Jamie.'

Grandad smiled. 'Yes, well, I was going to. Why do you think we come here in the first place? And what do you want to know, exactly?'

'There's a mystery about Ebenezer. You've got a secret.'

Grandad suddenly put on his 'cagey' look. 'Well, secrets is secrets. And if you lets 'em out of the bag at all, you lets them out a bit at a time. I told you who Ebenezer was, and some of what he did. He designed engines – he was a genius.'

'But something went wrong . . . that's what you said.'

'Ah, it did. I told you I didn't know the rights of it. There was that bust up with George Stephenson in Newcastle, an' Ebenezer come south. They reckons he had a revolutionary loco up his sleeve – something that would have changed the history of the railways, maybe. But it was never built.'

'Why not?' Grandad didn't answer at once, so Phil frowned, trying to work out the reason for himself. 'I suppose there wasn't enough money. I mean, it would have cost a lot to build a new engine. Perhaps George Stephenson wouldn't help, and that's why there was a bust up. . . .'

Grandad smiled with his lips but his eyes were watchful. 'Maybe you're right about the bust up. I told you, Ebenezer was a hothead, an' getting a fit of the sulks because he couldn't get his own way up at Newcastle, then coming down here hoping for a better deal, yes, that could be. But it wasn't money, boy. Ebenezer had pots of money – the family's always been sure of that. When he arrived in Deptford, Ebenezer was a wealthy man. He could have built the engine out of his own pocket.'

'Then . . . why didn't he?'

'Nobody knows, boy. Perhaps that doesn't matter any more. There's something else that does.'

A pigeon waddled across the gravel path between the tombs. Grandad absently gave it a gentle poke with the tip of his stick, and the pigeon pecked at it.

Phil's eyes widened. 'The money! What happened to Ebenezer's money?'

Grandad grinned. 'That's the ticket! I knew you wouldn't be long asking that. Well, that's the point – nobody knows. He didn't spend it. Least, we can't see how he could have. All we knows is that down here he got himself a reputation as a recluse and a miser. He shut himself away and behaved like a penniless beggar, an' his family went hungry more'n likely. And in the end, Ebenezer went off his head – an' then he died.'

Phil peered at the inscriptions again. 'Two years after Jamie . . .' Phil went on thinking, the ideas swirling in his head. 'If he had a lot of money, wouldn't he have kept it in a bank?'

'If he'd done that, boy, it wouldn't have got lost. No, if Ebenezer had money, he hid it.'

Grandad's look was tantalizing. Phil gasped, 'Not – not in our attic?'

The old man seemed to stop breathing. 'What do you know about the attic?' And his voice hardened.

Phil blushed. 'Only . . . that you have secrets up there. Things you won't tell me about!'

Grandad's moustache twitched. 'You're a sharp one! Well, that yarn about Cobber McCoy couldn't be expected to hold water for ever. Anyway, there ain't any money in the attic. It ain't anywhere in the house. I should know. I've been hunting for it for fifty years.'

'Then . . .'

'Then nothing! I'll tell you this much, though. If there *is* money, it's for you – every penny. Nobody else is going to lay hands on it, an' there are nosy parkers in this world who'd grab it if they could get their hooks on it. That's why I don't talk much about it – to anybody, not even you.'

'But what makes you still think Ebenezer's money is hidden somewhere? I mean . . .'

'You think maybe it's just a lot of family talk – a sort of legend? Well, yes – partly it is. But there are other ways of knowing, or guessing.'

'And the attic?'

'Never mind the attic. You're not to go near that attic till I say so! If you find out things too soon, and the nosy parkers get to hear . . . You just keep on with your book learning, and keep away from the attic, d'you hear, boy?'

Grandad's manner was almost frightening. Phil couldn't meet his gaze. 'Of course I hear.' His own voice was resentful and formal.

But in a moment Grandad, without speaking, laid a hand on Phil's shoulder. For a little while they stood together – the boy, the old man and the angel. Phil didn't take his eyes from the grave. Down there lay all that was left of the old Bensons. Ebenezer . . . genius, madman – miser? Old Stephen, Sarah, Elizabeth, Timothy and Maggie. . . . What secrets had they taken with them?

And Jamie Benson, whose short, white bones lay under all the rest . . . why had he died so young?

The angel's great wings seemed to quiver, the marble

lips smiled with watchful compassion. But the tranquil eyes were fixed on the grave, not on Phil.

Phil shivered. Grandad grunted, and the sound was like the ragged end of a thought. They both turned slowly away and went home.

The weeks passed. Christmas came and went. After that sudden flow of revelations at the churchyard Grandad dried up. There was no mention of the attic, not a word about Ebenezer's missing fortune. But sometimes Phil wondered . . . when Grandad had referred to 'nosy parkers' who might want to lay their hands on the hidden money, had he been thinking of someone *special*?

Grandad's big secret stayed hidden and was never discussed between them. But he still, sometimes, told Phil things about the viaduct, so that Phil himself began to go down there alone, full of dreams, making his own discoveries.

Then, early in January, he met Andy Smith.

3 The wasteland and the cave

Andy Smith was the new boy at school, having moved to Deptford from another part of London. His father was a radio officer in the Merchant Navy. Quite by chance he was put next to Phil in class and a friendship grew quickly – surprisingly, since they were so different. Or perhaps being different helped; each had qualities the other admired and envied.

Andy was quick witted, practical, down-to-earth. He had the freckled face that often goes with ginger hair, a chunky strength and an adventurous spirit. He was not without imagination, however, and when Phil, without meaning to boast, told him that he came from a long line of railway people and that one of his ancestors had been a 'real pioneer', Andy's face was as bright as a torch. He seized upon Phil's information and shook it, like a kitten shaking a ball of wool. '*What* pioneer?'

'Well, he isn't in a history book.' It sounded like an apology.

One Saturday morning Phil took Andy along the viaduct path and showed him what he nowadays called the 'Wasteland'. He'd promised to show his secrets, and Andy was all for secrets. But Phil held everything back until they had crossed the first of the footbridges out of the streets and had reached the desolate area near the canal. Here was the land Grandad had shown him, a land inhabited by half-wild cats, foraging dogs, rats, pigeons and sparrows—the area Phil called the 'Wasteland'. Clouds heavy with threatening snow hung in the sky and the muddy pools gleamed a metallic grey.

At the top of the second footbridge they paused, looking

down at the junk heaps; car bodies abandoned to decay, empty cans, broken barrels and rusty rails which once had borne long-dead trains. When they descended the steps their feet crunched on fragments of broken glass. At the bottom, Phil ran on until he reached a particular arch of ancient brickwork. When Andy caught up, Phil's face was mysteriously jubilant, and his finger was pointing at the wall inside the arch.

Andy didn't see anything at first. 'What are we supposed to be looking at?'

'Use your eyes!'

Andy peered closer. Then he read out what he saw – the faintest of scratchings in the brickwork, less than four feet above the long grass under the arch: ' "J.B. 1843" . . . who carved that?'

'A boy,' said Phil, his voice awed, as though they were the footprints of a dinosaur. 'One of my ancestors, Jamie Benson. His father was Ebenezer Benson, the genius, who worked up north with George Stephenson.'

'Cor! The one who built the Rocket?'

'Yes, and my ancestor used to design engines, too.'

'Who, Jamie?'

'No, Ebenezer. There were a lot of old Bensons. Jamie was one of his sons, and there was another called Timothy, who was *my* grandad's grandad. And there was a sister named Elizabeth, too. They're all buried in the church yard, and I've seen their names on the tombstone. . . .'

'Hold on! You're talking too fast, and it's so complicated.'

'Well, my grandad says Jamie carved his initials on the wall not all that long after the viaduct was built. He was ten, then, because he died when he was eleven and that was a year later. Have you got it?'

Andy scowled uncertainly. 'More or less. Why isn't your Ebenezer in the history books?'

'We don't really know. Grandad says he went crazy – Ebenezer, I mean. And he fell out with George Stephenson, and sulked, and came down here, and then he was a miser and a recluse. . . .'

'What's a recluse?'

'A sort of hermit, I think. Anyway, he built our house, and he wanted to build a new kind of engine, but . . .'

'But what?'

'Oh – nothing.'

Phil suddenly realized that in his wild rush of enthusiasm he was telling Andy too much. He was rather glad when Andy lost interest in the initials and turned away. 'Is that all you meant – about secrets?'

'Of course not! Come on.'

At the far end of the path the viaduct, its brick feet striding into the borough of Bermondsey, gathered other branches to itself and became wide and thick and complex. Phil led the way through a short paved road into a rubbish-filled space forming a triangle between two sets of arches. On their right was a rough, grassed embankment rising half-way up to the parapets, whilst upon their left the arches were enclosed by corrugated iron frontages with smaller rectangular doors secured by rusty padlocks which bore every sign of long disuse.

Phil stopped again at one of these doors which was almost concealed behind a heap of garbage from which grew tall, spiky weeds with stems as thick as snakes. He gave Andy a bright, quizzical glance, then felt in his trouser pocket and produced a penknife. Using a broken blade he began picking away at the rust-coated screws holding the padlock hasp, doing this expertly and quickly as though he'd often done it before. Within a few seconds the screws had dropped into his palm, and, to Andy's astonishment, the door squeaked open outwards.

'Crafty, eh?' gasped Andy.

The Viaduct

The door would open only a few inches before becoming fouled against the rubbish heap. Phil squeezed through the opening, leaving Andy to follow. When they were inside, Phil pulled the door behind them, leaving the merest suggestion of daylight. Andy blinked, trying to get his eyes used to the gloom.

The curved dome of the arch loomed over their heads like the inside of a whale's stomach. On each side were dusty, wooden shelves, fitted to follow the curvature of the brickwork – shelves like the ribs of the whale. Large, rectangular packing cases occupied practically every inch of space. There were black stencilled numbers and letters visible on the nearest of these. One or two had broken open, or been tampered with.

'What's in them?' asked Andy, his voice hushed.

'I'll show you.' Phil pushed a hand into one of the cases and yanked at some fabric. He held a garment closer to the chink in the doorway. It was a dark blue tunic, faded, smelling of mildew and with holes and tears gaping. 'Old railway uniforms. There are caps, too – all pretty ancient.'

'Your grandad show you?'

Phil grinned. 'No fear! Even he doesn't know about this place. Nobody does, so far as I know. Other kids come by, sometimes, but none has ever touched those screws. I'd know if they had.'

'It would make a smashing den,' breathed Andy.

'I call it the Cave.'

A train passed overhead. The terrifying sound was like a dozen claps of thunder. The dome throbbed on and on ... thunder, or a giant wave smashing against an unseen cliff. Excitement gleamed in Andy's eyes. The boys sat side by side on a low shelf.

When it was quiet again, Andy said, 'Tell us more about that ancestor of yours – the genius one. What was his name again?'

'Ebenezer. Well . . . all right.'

Phil did not, then, mention the attic and Grandad's secretiveness about what was up there. But he told a lot of other things. It was so easy to talk on and on, because they were alone in that strange place and Andy was his first real friend. So he dug in his memory for other things Grandad had told him about the old Bensons, especially Ebenezer. 'I told you how he quarrelled with George Stephenson in Newcastle . . . well, when he came to Deptford he was manager of a locomotive works. Grandad thinks the place wasn't far from here – somewhere in the viaduct arches. And you know what? Ebenezer was a rich man. . . .'

'A miser, you said.'

'Yes . . . and we don't know what happened to his money. We think he hid it, and Grandad's been looking for it for fifty years.'

'Cor!' Andy scowled. 'You don't reckon he's having you on?'

'What? Are you calling my grandad a fibber?'

Andy stirred uneasily. He noticed that Phil had clenched his fists. 'No, but . . . well, you've only his word for it. And he sounds pretty old, and eccentric. About those initials . . .'

'What about them?'

'You don't *know* that your Jamie Benson carved them. It might have been some other kid, mucking about – a more modern kid.'

Phil couldn't see any sense in this wilful doubting. He had not learned, yet, that Andy always doubted things unless there were scientific proof. Phil wished, again, that he had not told so much. He wanted to undo all the telling, because Andy's doubting made him feel uncomfortable and unsure. 'Look, you won't let on about this – to anybody else? It's really a family secret.'

Andy ritually whipped two fingers across his throat. 'Of

course not.' He waited for another train to finish its thundering, then he said, 'This is a smashing place. We ought to have a table and some proper chairs, and I could bring some candles.'

Phil had not thought of candles. When they came out of the cave, the wintry world glared unnaturally bright. Phil carefully replaced the screws, then they hurried back along the deserted path. Andy chatted on about how they would furnish the Cave.

The main effect of this first real conversation with Andy was to make Phil impatient to learn the truth about Ebenezer and his hidden money. All he'd had so far were hints, and yarns, and warnings not to go near the attic. He wanted more – much more.

Andy's doubting had worried him, partly because it tallied with what Mrs Partridge had said. She'd referred to Ebenezer's affairs as 'that old tale', and told Phil that what Grandad said must be taken with 'a pinch of salt'. Andy had, in a way, been right about everything. What proof was there that any of Grandad's stories were true? Only a few names on a tombstone, a faded inscription on a brick wall – and they weren't proof.

Of course, Andy didn't yet know about the attic, but would it have made any difference if Phil had told him? Hardly. Phil didn't know much about it himself, beyond the fact that whatever was there had some connection with the mystery. He badly wanted to take a peep, perhaps find something tangible that he could take to his new friend and say, 'Look, this *proves* it's true!'

But what counted was his promise to Grandad. Phil shrank from breaking what had been practically a sacred vow. And yet, a few days later, Phil did learn a little – quite by chance – and without having to cheat.

He sensed that he had not been asleep long when a

single, jarring thump woke him. He sat up, bewildered for a moment, not knowing what had caused it. Vivid blue flares streaked across the tall rectangle of his window and he could hear the sizzling sound of an electric train's pick-up shoes trying to cope with newly fallen snow on the live rail.

Then . . . silence. Oddly, Phil did not think of the attic. His first thought was that Grandad had suffered some mishap – dropped off to sleep, perhaps, and fallen out of his chair. He might need help. He got out of bed, opened his door, and would have walked straight on, bare-footed, along the landing to the living-room. Then, what he saw made him shrink, half-guiltily, back through his own doorway.

Grandad's wooden steps bestraddled the landing and, above, the attic hatchway was open like a black mouth. The living-room door was ajar and the light switched on.

A metal trunk, perhaps two feet long and half as wide, stood open on the table. It was a dull black and looked

battered and old. Beside it, arranged roughly in small heaps, were rolls of yellowish paper, loose sheets, envelopes and a few little flat boxes, or cases, covered with some kind of fabric like lizard skin.

Arranged askew near the edge of the table were some books, and it was a number of these which, apparently, had toppled to the floor. Grandad, his back turned to Phil, was in the process of picking them up. They were thick books with heavy bindings of leather, one lying with its pages splayed out, the stout spine uppermost.

Phil took all this in at a glimpse, then bobbed back into his room and softly closed the door.

4 Word from Uncle Ern

Straight after school next day the boys roughly furnished the Cave, finding a rickety old basket-work table from a rubbish heap and a couple of boxes for seats. Andy lit the first of his candles and the new glow threw their shadows big against the packing cases.

Phil told him the rest – almost everything there was to tell – watching Andy anxiously to see how he was taking it. A train arrived neatly at the end of the story, giving Andy time to mull it over, biting his fingernails. 'You're sure you didn't dream what happened last night?'

'Of course I'm sure! There was this trunk, and loads of papers and books.'

'What, no doubloons, or pieces of eight?'

Phil glared and Andy's grin vanished. 'And you reckon the stuff has something to do with your Ebenezer's money, a miser's hoard?'

Phil sighed exasperatedly. 'You make it all sound like something out of a soppy story.'

'I didn't *mean* to. Suppose there is some money . . . how much would it be?'

Phil had never thought about this. It had never seemed important. A hundred pounds? A thousand? More?

The dusty dome of the Cave throbbed again, then Andy said, 'It would be in gold sovereigns, I expect. I don't think they had pound notes in those days.' This was the sort of general knowledge that Andy was so good at. 'What would happen if you found it?'

'Grandad said it would be mine. He's got this idea about sending me to college later on. He wants me to be an engineer.'

'You could do that without finding the money. Nowadays, if you're brainy enough for college you get a government grant.'

Phil shrugged. 'Grandad wouldn't think of that.'

Andy stared thoughtfully at the candle flame, his eyes bright in its flicker. It was hard to tell what he believed. Was this, for him, just the beginning of a game – an imagining? 'All right. There are papers, and books ... let's call them Documents X. And they contain hidden clues about where Ebenezer the Miser hid his gold. ...' He nibbled his fingers again. 'But in that case, it's funny your grandad hasn't solved the puzzle by now – if there is a solution. I mean, according to you he's been taking crafty look-sees in that attic for ages – at least, ever since you were a titch, and he kidded you along about the dwarf. ... Say, d'you think he does know where the money is, but won't tell until you're older? After all, he's had loads of time to read what's in those books.'

Phil said, yielding his final secret, 'Grandad *can't* read – much. You swear you won't tell? He's jolly touchy about it. It's not that he's daft, he just never had a proper chance to learn. ...'

Andy banged the table and the candle jumped in its tin lid. 'Then don't you see? That explains a lot – why he's been hiding Documents X, waiting for you to grow up. He's made you do all that homework, not only because he wants you to go to college, but so's you can tell him what's in those books. He's scared stiff of nosy parkers, you said, and won't trust anybody else.'

Phil nodded. 'Yes, I'd already guessed that – or partly.' His look was half pleading. 'Andy, you do believe all this, don't you? You do think ...'

'I think it's time we took a peep at Documents X! I bet we could read them, between us.'

'But ... it can't be done. I promised Grandad not to

look in the attic.' Andy shrugged irritatingly. Phil went on, weakly: 'Besides, he probably keeps the trunk locked, and I haven't the foggiest where the key is.'

'Have you tried looking for it? Anyway, why don't you ask your grandad – straight out – to let you borrow some of the books? They'll be yours one day. Aren't you the last of the Bensons?'

Phil somehow liked that phrase – last of the Bensons. It had an exciting, challenging ring, like *The Last of the Mohicans*.

'I'll think it over,' he said.

Andy shrugged again, as though thinking was the most useless of all accomplishments.

The more Phil thought over Andy's suggestion, the more the butterflies fluttered in his tummy. And he was right – it couldn't be done. He persuaded himself that even if he were to try and get a closer look at the contents of the trunk, he wouldn't manage it without making a row and being caught out. Suppose he did succeed; what would he learn that he didn't know already? Very little, because he would not have time for more than a quick glance, and he could hardly cart off any of the documents to Andy without Grandad's permission. Phil could not imagine the old man granting anything of the sort. Besides, if he asked, Grandad would think he had been spying on purpose.

Was there a key? Phil, piecing together his memories – the trunk on the table, the papers beside it and the heavy books being retrieved by a stooping Grandad – couldn't be sure. But, if he had no intention of tackling the trunk by himself, that hardly mattered, for the moment. Phil tried to stop such details whirling endlessly in his mind and concentrated on more important wonderings.

As Andy had said, Grandad had had years in which to

try and unravel the secrets of 'Documents X', so why, if he couldn't read them, hadn't he given up the struggle long ago? Mere curiosity, or stubbornness? Or were there other things to look at, things which Grandad *could* understand, and which he hoped might, if he went on doggedly studying them, lead him to Ebenezer's secret?

Just how long had Grandad known of the trunk's existence? Since he'd been a young man – a boy, even? No, because then there would have been other people living in the house, members of the family who *could* read, and therefore would have known what the documents contained. The trunk must have lain hidden, perhaps under heaps of junk, and he'd discovered it accidentally during some upheaval when the attic was tidied. Or had he found it somewhere else in the house and heaved it into the attic on his bony old shoulders? And once he had got it there, where he could most easily reach it, had a search through the musty pages enabled him to piece together a few bits of their mystery? Surely, yes, otherwise how would he know that Documents X had anything more than curiosity value? And having guessed that in some way they must point to the whereabouts of Ebenezer's money, perhaps Grandad had made fruitless searches of his own – probing into dark corners, tapping hollow walls with his stick, suffering endless and lonely disappointments. . . .

There were so many questions, so many things Phil didn't know. The questions buzzed in his head during the rest of the week and it was Saturday morning when, like a thunderbolt, the biggest guess of all flashed into his mind. *He was suddenly sure of whom Grandad was afraid.*

Andy was away visiting relations and Grandad was out walking. Phil leaned on the sill of his bedroom window, looking out. A new fall of night snow was already melting. The houses opposite crowded close like a flock of geese shedding their feathers, and when a train rumbled on the viaduct, unfreezing lips of snow plopped from gutters into the street.

Andy had called Phil 'the last of the Bensons', but that wasn't strictly true. There were, as the snapshots showed, Bensons of all shapes and sizes still living somewhere. Grandad had mentioned their infrequent visits, and Phil could remember none of them.

But there was *Uncle Ernest*, Grandad's elder son of whom the old man always spoke in such tones of bitterness. 'Him and that flighty wife of his, your Aunt Luce. . . .'

Uncle Ern had been brought up in the Benson house, and he and Aunt Luce once lived near by and had called at various times after their marriage. If Uncle Ern was the sort of person Grandad said he was, mightn't he have known, or guessed, something of Grandad's secret? Was he, or he and Aunt Luce, the 'nosy parker' Grandad had referred to – the unnamed person who might 'get to hear' what was in the attic?

Phil wondered whether Mrs Partridge, so helpful with information when carefully questioned, would help him now. He wandered downstairs to the kitchen, where she was cutting up meat.

'Mrs Partridge, you know my Uncle Ernest?'

'No, and I can't say that I want to, from what I've heard.'

'What have you heard?'

'Well, perhaps it's not for me to tattle. He led your grandad a regular dance, one way and another.'

'He's . . . bad?'

'Weak and greedy, more like it. Always in some sort of money bother. A great one for get-rich-quick schemes that never come off – but maybe that's just talk.'

'Where is he now?'

Mrs Partridge's knife paused. 'I haven't the least idea.

45

Your grandad never mentions him to me. They didn't get
on, you know.'

Phil nodded and tried to make his next question sound
casual. 'When Uncle Ern and Aunt Luce came here, were
there rows – about anything special?'

'That was before my time, love. They don't come any
more, and the way your grandad feels maybe it's just as
well. Now, if you've finished the quiz show perhaps you'd
be a dear and pop the kettle on. Your grandad should be
back soon, then we'll all have a nice cup of tea. I expect the
silly old chap's got his feet wet in all that slush. . . .'

There was no way of guessing, then, how rapidly and un-
happily events were to turn out. To begin with, Mrs
Partridge's fears proved all too well grounded. Grandad
had got his feet wet, he caught a cold, and within a day or
two it turned into bronchitis. Much against his will, Mrs
Partridge made him go to bed and sent for the doctor. For
several days Phil spent all his free time reading to the old
man and playing endless games of ludo and snakes and
ladders, with the boards propped tilted on the bedclothes
so that the pieces were always getting mixed and Grandad
grew petulant and accused Phil of cheating.

Grandad's voice practically disappeared, so there wasn't
as much talk as usual. Often he fell asleep in the middle of
a game, and it was during one of these spells that Phil
spotted something he had never noticed before. On Grandad's bedside table, amongst the coins from his pockets and
half hidden by a bottle of medicine, was his old-fashioned
watch and chain, attached to which was a small, ornate
brass key. Phil had no means of knowing, yet he was sure
that it was the key to the trunk. He eyed it with fascination,
but did not touch it.

The doctor called a second time and seemed satisfied
with Grandad's progress, and then, one bitter morning with

ice on the windows, the postman delivered a card addressed to Grandad. Mrs Partridge brought it upstairs and handed it to Phil, her face blank. Phil looked at the back. 'Crumbs!' he whispered, out on the landing. 'Did you see who it's from?'

'Yes . . . you'll have to tell him, I suppose.'

Phil took the postcard to Grandad, who was sitting up waiting for his breakfast. He was immediately curious, for he so rarely received mail. 'Where's it from?'

'Luton.' Phil had read the postmark first.

Grandad snatched it out of his hand, then peered, angry but uncomprehending, at the spidery writing. The old joke sounded forced. 'Haven't got me specs . . . you'd better read it.'

Phil read the message: ' "Luce and me thought of popping over one day next week. Hope you're well, Ern." '

'Is that all?' Grandad shrank back against the pillows, his face turning from grey to red. 'Well, I *ain't* well . . . an' what do those two want, coming here out of the blue? If they've got ideas about . . .'

The husky sentence ended in mystery. Grandad threw the card to the bottom of the bed then, when Mrs Partridge had brought the tray, nibbled at his breakfast in silence.

He scarcely looked up when Phil, setting out for school, said good-bye.

It was just after morning break when Phil was told there had been a telephone message from Mrs Partridge, and he was to go home at once. His grandad had had some kind of accident and had been rushed to hospital.

A teacher drove him home. Mrs Partridge was at the door. 'Now, there's no need to be upset . . . he may be all right. The doctor came and acted very quickly, but they're afraid of pneumonia, because your grandad's broken some ribs. He fell . . .'

'Fell?'

Mrs Partridge thanked the teacher and drew Phil indoors. 'I shall never forgive myself for leaving him, but how could I have guessed . . . ? He was in his bed, and he seemed quite comfy though he was brooding about that card from your uncle. I was down in the kitchen when I heard this thump. I ran up, and he was lying across the landing. He'd fetched those steps of his, and . . . oh, Phil! He'd opened that hatch thing and fallen off the steps. He was conscious, but talking funny . . . about the snow melting, and a leak over his bed. He seemed to want to explain everything. . . . I think he was delirious. Now, what on earth had got into him, to make him do a thing like that?'

Phil knew . . . or thought he knew. He felt frightened, and miserable, and dreadfully sick.

Mrs Partridge, usually so calm and practical, fingered her apron anxiously. 'I hope I did the right thing, Phil . . . the doctor said we should. I've sent a telegram to your uncle. The address was on that card, and . . . well, I suppose he ought to know, especially as he was coming next week anyway. . . .'

5 A small, brass key

'It's funny,' said Uncle Ern, 'how small this garden seems whenever I come back to it. Your dad and me used to play football out here when we was kids. Can remember busting the window, over there in the kitchen. Got a right clip round the ear by the old man. . . .'

It was the day after the accident, and Phil had been excused from school because they were all going to the hospital that afternoon. The snow had gone and the solitary hawthorn tree was as black as soot against the decaying boundary wall.

'I suppose I asked for it,' went on Uncle Ern, reminiscently. 'Was always a bit wild as a kid. They tell me you take after your dad?'

Phil nodded. He knew that Uncle Ern had brought him out here while the family doctor, who had just called, talked with Mrs Partridge and Aunt Luce indoors. The doctor had been in touch with the hospital, and his blank, professional expression had not deceived Phil. Phil knew that Grandad was not expected to live much longer.

'Not much of a dump, is it, when you come to look?' Uncle Ern bared his teeth at the thin, tall old house. He was shorter, even slighter, than Grandad. He resembled him, but his face was sharper, more of a rodent's. He had a thin, tobacco-stained moustache and he was forever stroking his ear with his thumb. 'Your aunt and me, we've a nice little place up in Luton. Struck a bit lucky with a spot of business only last year. Nice piece of land to go with it and all. . . .' Pale blue eyes focused on Phil for a moment, as though questions were already waiting to come from behind them. His glance flicked back to the windows.

'Ugly old heap of bricks ... I bet, if houses could talk, this one could tell us some tales, eh? I bet it could tell us some tales. ...'

Phil said nothing, feeling awkward, waiting only to go back in. He had not expected to take to Uncle Ern, and he hadn't. The man was so anxious to make excuses for himself, as though he wanted Phil to think well of him. His habit of repeating himself was a kind of thrusting anxiety to make himself understood: 'I expect the old man told you a few things about me, but there were faults on both sides, sonny. Oh, there were faults on both sides. ...'

There was a small argument about all of them visiting Grandad. Uncle Ern jerked his head towards Mrs Partridge, when she was just out of earshot. 'The old chap won't want a crowd. Just the family, not hangers on.'

'Mrs Partridge has been more like a family to him than we have,' replied Aunt Luce, and Phil glanced at her in surprise. She was not a bit the vulgar, flighty person he had expected to meet : she was small, rather mousy and timid. Yet her eyes kindled when she spoke to Uncle Ern, who shrugged, rolled a cigarette, and didn't argue further. Aunt Luce gave Phil a shy, sympathetic smile.

The Bensons owned an old car with badly pitted paint-work and Uncle Ern drove casually and carelessly through the wet streets. The women bought flowers and fruit at a stall near the hospital gates, then they went through and joined a small crowd in the waiting-room. As not more than two visitors were allowed at a time, Uncle Ern told Aunt Luce to take Mrs Partridge through first. 'I'll take the boy in with me, later,' he said.

Phil wondered whether there was some kind of plot in his uncle's mind. Was he imagining things, or did Uncle Ern want to be present when Phil saw Grandad? Did he think that the dying man might tell Phil something that he, Uncle Ern, wished to hear as well?

Uncle Ern glared at the NO SMOKING notice and said, 'They may not let you in, you know. "Children admitted at the Sister's discretion" – that's what it says on the board. Anyway, it's unlikely to make much difference. From what the doctor said, your grandad won't recognize anybody – too far gone. Well, he's had his life. . . .' His off-hand air showed that he'd not intended his remarks to be cruel or unfeeling.

Phil watched some younger children tumbling about on the seat opposite. 'Now behave,' said their mother. 'Else the nice nurses won't let you see your grandad.'

Phil felt the tears smart in his eyes and bit his lip.

At last the corridor doors swung open. The middle-aged Sister appeared, accompanied by a youthful, friendly faced doctor in a white coat, Mrs Partridge, a handkerchief to her mouth, and Aunt Luce, looking pale and bewildered.

Uncle Ern started to his feet, and the doctor smiled hesitantly. 'He's asked especially to see his grandson first, and alone. I think we should respect his wishes.' Uncle Ern looked put out, but he sat down.

In the ward, Grandad lay surrounded by screens on castors. His eyes were open, dimly fixed on Phil as he self-consciously made his way slowly between the green curtains. 'Hullo, boy!' Phil took the outstretched hand. It felt clammy and cold, but the grasp was tight as it drew him nearer. For an instant Grandad seemed so natural, only a little unwell, as he had been a few days before when they'd argued over their dice games on the bedclothes at home. Then with a sinking heart he realized that Grandad's naturalness was a waxen illusion, that he lay, near the end, summoning the last of his strength. 'Want to tell, you, boy . . . about what's in the attic. Should've told you long ago . . . should've trusted you. . . .'

Phil nodded, and the figure in the white bed became someone seen in a deep, shifting mist. Phil spoke of what he knew, of what he had seen, in quick, broken sentences, so that it was like a hurried confession.

Grandad understood most of it. The grip tightened and a smile touched his pale lips, and he said faintly, 'You're a smart boy, I always knew it. You'll know what to do, then, you and your chum, Andy . . . an' don't let your Uncle Ern find out nothing, not yet, boy. When . . . when you find the money, you can be fair with him, but no more'n that. . . .' Phil blinked away his tears and now he could see the new brightness in Grandad's eyes. 'You'll be a great engineer, boy . . . I always knew it . . . like . . . like old Ebenezer, eh?'

Then Grandad closed his eyes, and there was contentment drawing a veil across the wrinkled features, as if Phil – even Phil – was left far behind, and Grandad was keeping a tryst with the old Bensons. . . .

It was not until after the funeral that Phil and Andy met

at the Cave. Andy bit his nails anxiously, fumbling too long with the candle, not knowing what to say.

Then he said, 'Did – did it all go off all right?'

Phil sighed. 'It was pretty ghastly, but it's all over now – that part of things.'

'Suppose there were a lot of flowers?'

'Quite a lot. And all sorts of relations. It's funny, Andy, how they never bothered with us when Grandad was alive. Then . . . well, they all turned up wearing black and crying, as if they really *cared*.'

Andy had never been to a funeral. 'In some countries they *pay* people to cry at funerals.'

'Do they?' Phil added, disgustedly, 'But afterwards they all came back to the house and sat about, eating and drinking, as if it was a sort of party.'

'What's going to happen now – at home?'

'I don't know. Uncle Ern and Aunt Luce are still hanging about. They're going through Grandad's things. I'm sleeping downstairs in Mrs Partridge's spare room – she's offered to look after me while they see to this and that. I don't think they're sure what to do with me.'

Andy said, 'My mum said you could stay with us, for a while. Dad's not home all that much.'

'Thanks, Andy. That would be smashing, only . . . well, I overheard some talk and I think I might eventually have to live with my uncle and aunt.'

'Where, in Luton?'

'I don't know. It hasn't been sorted out, yet. I think Aunt Luce wants to go home to Luton, but Uncle Ern would sooner stay here. You see, the house is his, now, or it will be.'

'What about Mrs Partridge?'

'There's some talk of her going to live with her sister. She's always wanted to.'

'But she can't leave you with *them*.'

Phil smiled bleakly. 'Aunt Luce isn't bad. I think we'll get along. But Uncle Ern ...' He didn't finish that bit.

They hardly heard the train's thunder. After a moment Andy said, 'If he's going to go through your grandad's belongings, won't he turn out the attic and find the trunk?'

'Yes.'

'Then ... don't you care?'

'Of course I care. I don't know how yet, but I'm going to try and get the stuff and bring it here. At the hospital Grandad gave us permission to have it. Yes, I told him about you and everything. He said I wasn't to let Uncle Ern find the trunk, but I was to be fair to him when we found the money.'

'Give him some of it, he meant?'

'I expect so. He couldn't ... talk very much. Andy, I'm sure Uncle Ern guesses something. It was as if he'd sent that postcard, and was coming to see Grandad, because he knew about the money and was going to force Grandad to tell him where it was. And Grandad knew this would happen, too. Nobody else has guessed yet, but I'm sure that's why, when he got upset and delirious, he tried to reach the trunk. He was going to hide it somewhere fresh ... or so he thought.'

Andy nodded. 'But why didn't Uncle Ern come before? Why wait until now?'

'That's another thing that's been puzzling me. Perhaps, when he lived at the house, he heard the old family stories. Then, for some reason, he suddenly remembered them, and decided to come and try and find Ebenezer's hoard for himself. And I bet he won't give up till he succeeds.'

Andy whistled. 'Then we've got to move – fast. When are you going to bring the trunk?'

'It's going to be tricky. Uncle Ern and Aunt Luce sleep in Grandad's old bedroom so if I do it at night, they're almost sure to hear. And they always seem to be about during the day.'

'Did you ever find a key?'

Phil reached in his pocket. 'Yes. . . . I think it's the one.'

He let it lie on the palm of his hand, and they both looked.

Phil had obtained the key after their visit to the hospital. Occupied with more urgent matters, Mrs Partridge had not taken Grandad's watch and chain with his other things in the ambulance. It still lay on the bedside table, next to the coins, half-hidden by the medicine bottle. The old, yellowish dial of the watch was uppermost, the big hands stationary. The tiny second hand was still, too, like a stopped heart; but when Phil had disturbed the watch, it began to scuttle round its miniature dial.

Phil had wrenched the key from its metal spiral ring and thrust it into his pocket.

6 Night operation

After a bit, Phil began to go upstairs for most of his meals. He had the feeling that this was Aunt Luce's suggestion. One morning, at breakfast, she said, 'We don't want to upset your usual routine. You just tell me anything you don't like eating, and I'll do my best.'

Her small, drab figure darted about, anxious to please. It was difficult to know what she was really like, at first, but that was because she wanted to be accepted by Phil but was unsure how to go about it. She gave him lots of quick, hesitant little smiles, though her eyes were mostly uneasy and unhappy. She and Uncle Ern did not talk much in Phil's presence, but gradually Phil sensed that she was on his side.

Uncle Ern slouched in a chair, waiting to be served like a man in a restaurant. When Aunt Luce went down to consult Mrs Partridge about something he laid down his newspaper and gave Phil a penetrating look. 'You might be able to help us, son. How much did your grandad tell you about family affairs?'

Phil said carefully, 'Not much.'

Uncle Ern's pale eyes stared as he tried to gauge Phil's intelligence. He hadn't much idea what a ten-year-old boy could understand of grown-up concerns. 'It's about the old man's property, if you can call it that. We was wondering if he left a will. You know what a will is?'

'Yes.'

Uncle Ern opened a tin of tobacco and began manufacturing himself a cigarette. 'Going off sudden like that, he's left us a few problems, you might say. There's this house, for a start. And there's our little place up in Luton. Your aunt isn't keen on selling that. Then there's you. Mind, whatever happens, we'll see you're all right. We know our duty when we see it.'

He licked the cigarette paper, struck a match, and continued his steady gaze through a cloud of blue smoke. He was waiting for Phil to say something. Phil gave him no help.

'Not that a will matters much. I don't suppose your grandad ever made one. After all, the poor old codger didn't know a letter Z from a full stop, did he? But it don't make any difference. Oh, the legal-beagles might hum-and-ha a bit, but in time anything he left will come to me, seeing I'm his only surviving son, as the saying goes.'

Phil nodded, his legs screwed up tense under the table. Uncle Ern was driving at some point. Phil waited for it to arrive.

'Of course, I don't suppose your grandad had anything worth a brass farthing – only all this junk, and the house itself, for what that's worth. Then again, we could be wrong.'

He took a long pull at his cigarette then blew the smoke out slowly, watching to see what effect his last remark would have. When Phil still remained silent, he thumbed his ear and went on, 'Did he ever yarn to you about that old ancestor of ours? The one who was supposed to have been an inventor. *What* was his name?'

'Ebenezer . . .' Phil bit his lip and Uncle Ern's eyes gleamed.

'Ah, so you do know about him. Thought maybe you did. Reckon there's anything in that tale about him hiding some money?'

Phil felt himself blushing as he stammered, 'I – I don't know. Perhaps . . .'

Uncle Ern grinned unpleasantly. 'Perhaps you know more than you're letting on just now, eh? Well, there's no hurry. There're going to be some changes around here, sonny, but . . . there's no hurry.'

The boys talked at school next day, when Phil gave Andy an account of this. Afterwards Andy asked, 'Anything else happen?'

'Yes, a bit. I heard them talking again last night – they didn't know I was upstairs.' Phil didn't say whether his eavesdropping had been deliberate or not. 'They were having a bit of a squabble. Andy, you remember what I said about Uncle Ern guessing there was hidden money, and coming here to look for it?'

'Yes, and I asked why he'd come now, and not a long time ago.'

Phil was excited. 'I think I know why. He met somebody, and that somebody gave him some information.'

'But who?'

'Goodness knows. I think it was someone who knew Grandad, and then, recently, met Uncle Ern. The squabble last night started with Aunt Luce grumbling about the trains making a noise and keeping her awake at night. She said she wanted to go home. Uncle Ern sneered, and told her she'd have to put up with it because he wasn't leaving the house until he'd found what he called "the old codger's nest-egg". That's the way he talks about Grandad. . . .'

'Nest-egg,' mused Andy. 'That means money saved up, or stashed away . . . so he must think, like you once did, that your grandad actually *had* the money, and was hiding it. He doesn't know there's a trunk of books and stuff, but not the actual cash?'

'I don't think so – not yet.'

'What did your aunt say, then?'

'She got mad – she can, at times, with Uncle Ern. She said something about him being a fool to listen to what this mystery person said – I didn't hear a name – and that

it was just another of Uncle Ern's daft schemes. Then
Uncle Ern said, "It's here, somewhere. I reckon we'll get
rid of the Luton place, and that busybody downstairs . . ."
he meant Mrs Partridge, of course. ". . . and we'll take over
here. The house is still worth a bit, and ten to one there's
something stuffed away under the floor boards, or somewhere . . ." I couldn't hear the rest.'

Andy grinned unkindly. 'Meaning, you got your ear un-
stuck from the keyhole! So he hasn't thought of the attic,
yet. Phil, you've got to get the trunk . . . let's meet at the
Cave tonight and work out how to do it. It shouldn't be
that difficult, if you have a bit of gump!'

The meeting was, after all, short and acrimonious. Andy's
idea of a plan was that Phil should make a clean, bold
assault on the attic, grab the trunk, and make a run for it
to the Cave. At least, that's what it amounted to. When
Phil wouldn't agree, Andy called him 'windy'. Phil said it
was all very well for him to talk, he didn't have to do it.
In the end Phil would not discuss the plan that had begun
to form in his mind, but merely promised that, unless some
disaster defeated him, he would tackle the trunk on Friday
night. He had a way of hiding the contents until Saturday
morning, but he didn't tell Andy about this until later.

Several days passed in suspense. On each of them Phil
rushed home from school, wondering if Uncle Ern had got
round to searching the attic. There was always the frightening possibility that he might start wondering about Grandad's fall. So far, he had evidently accepted the generally
held view that the sick old man had, in his delirium, been
worried about a leak in the roof.

On Wednesday, Phil took a second look at something he
had only recently noticed. It was a battered old chest-of-
drawers which Mrs Partridge must have dumped at the foot
of the garden after a clear-out. Phil asked if he could have it.

'Whatever for?'

'Our camp.' Grown-ups understood about camps.

'It'll take a bit of carrying.'

'Andy's got a cart.'

On Friday, Phil collected less cumbersome objects together and hid them under the bed. A torch, a length of thin, nylon cord he'd swapped at school for a set of picture cards; a torch, and a copy of the local railway and bus timetable. He had decided, after all, that it would be best not to try and manhandle the trunk which would make an awkward clatter if he banged it about, but remove the contents first. Besides, the drawers of Mrs Partridge's discarded chest were very narrow. . . .

Keeping awake that night was not too difficult. He read, studied his timetable and listed the trains he wanted. Then he made up stories about the pictures on Mrs Partridge's spare-bedroom walls.

At nine o'clock he was able to check his clock by the time-pips on the radio upstairs. Over an hour passed after that, dreadfully slowly, then at last there were the sounds of movement . . . running water, the closing of doors.

At half past ten Mrs Partridge went into her own bedroom. Not long afterwards the radio upstairs was switched off in the middle of a popular song and, in due course, Phil heard the squeak of springs as someone climbed into bed. Then, a deepening silence – except for the regular passage of trains on the viaduct.

On average the trains took about half a minute to traverse the stretch of viaduct which passed the house. During those precious seconds, the whole dwelling trembled to its foundations, and every smaller sound would be engulfed in the thunder of steel-shod wheels. Only during such brief moments would Phil move, swift as a lizard, about his quest.

He decided to start with the eleven-twenty up-train, which stopped at Deptford station. Its slowing down would give him a little extra time for getting upstairs – the vital first part of his plan. When the time approached, he checked that the little brass key was safely wedged beneath the handkerchief in his pyjama pocket, zipped on his old anorak and whipped the outer cover from his pillow. He rammed the nylon cord into one of his pockets and gripped the torch.

The train was arriving. Even before the house felt the first tremor of its approach, Phil was through the door and heading for the foot of the stairs. The walls were shaking nicely by the time he was on the staircase, taking two treads at a time, then gaining the landing. He even managed to reach the kitchen recess and remove the steps before, later than he'd dared hope, the sounds died away and his quickened heart-beat throbbed like a drum in the quietness.

Phil panted, seeing specks of light swimming in the darkness ... then came the second train. Guardedly using his torch, he got the steps into position beneath the attic hatch, had shinned up them, pushed open the square of wood – and was squatting on the ledge before silence returned once more.

Now was the moment of crisis. ... If Phil had miscalculated, if the Bensons were not asleep – had been kept awake by the trains, perhaps and had overheard suspicious sounds. ... But the bedroom door remained firmly closed; there was no tell-tale appearance of a strip of light beneath. Reassuringly, even from his high perch, Phil could hear Uncle Ern's snores.

A cat squealed on the roof. The wind moaned like a murmuring voice. ... Trains, at this time of night, were growing scarce. Phil remembered that he had some time to wait. He played the torch on the cross-beams and rafters, saw the metal trunk and reached for his key. It fitted, but was stiff to turn. Phil sweated, wondering whether, after all, it was the right key ... then, to his immense relief it creaked round and he was able to open the lid.

He did not stop to examine the contents, merely hauled them out with reasonable care and stuffed them into the pillow case. He suddenly thought of Santa Claus, then, with a lump in his throat, of Grandad, and Cobber McCoy and the terrible Toby ...

Next he looped the cord in a firm slip knot around the neck of the pillow case. He eased the shapeless, unwieldy bundle as near the hatch as he dared. He wished he had a watch, the clock would have been too cumbersome. But he remembered that the next fast down-train should be almost due.

When the throbbing began he was panicky for a moment – he had trouble shifting the bundle. It seemed to be wedged between two of the cross-beams. By the time he got it free, the train had been shaking the house for half its allotted time, and he had wasted it! Too hurriedly he pushed the pillow case through the hatch, pressed his slippered feet against a cross-beam to take the strain and lowered his burden. It was heavier than he thought. The cord ripped through his hands, burning the palms. And, to Phil's horror, the swinging bundle struck the top of the ladder. He dimly saw the steps start to totter to and fro, leisurely, like a man on stilts. Too soon, the train thundered away, and voices rose from the bedroom: a few grunts from Uncle Ern, followed by a querulous complaint from Aunt Luce.

Now what was Phil to do? The next train, his memory told him, was not due for twenty minutes. He'd counted on completing the operation by now. And here he was, squatting in the attic with the pillow case still pivoting slowly and caressing the top of the steps. He dared not lower it farther, yet.

He tied the other end of the cord round his leg, leaving his hands free. He suddenly thought of the trunk, gaping

open, an inviter of questions when Uncle Ern eventually discovered it. He grabbed some old clothing that had once been used to lag water pipes, and stuffed that into the trunk, closing and relocking it.

Then, sheer luck saw him out of his dilemma. The house started to shake, and Phil, hardly able to believe it, realized that a goods train not scheduled in his timetable was rumbling up from Greenwich. A big diesel, too, by the sound of it.

Phil waited till it was near, then, making a final check round, allowed the bundle to ease itself to the landing floor, and climbed back through on to the steps platform, lowering the hatch behind him.

The thunder of the diesel lasted out the rest of his adventure: replacing the steps, heaving the weighty pillow case downstairs and through the kitchen, easing the bolts . . .

Frost silvered the hawthorn tree and chilly moonlight put a gleam on the handles of the old chest-of-drawers tilted on the rubbish heap. Phil forced open the two bottom drawers and emptied the pillow case into them. He shook the dust, as best he could, from the pillow case. Then, as he crept back into the house a last worry nagged at him. Suppose it rained, or snowed . . . but the stars winked encouragingly.

At breakfast Phil yawned several times. Uncle Ern eyed him thoughtfully over the top of his paper. 'What d'you reckon to do on Saturdays?'

'Oh . . . nothing special.'

'Maybe, later on, you can help us to go through your grandad's things.'

'Yes . . . okay.'

Aunt Luce came in. Although he slept downstairs, it was she who made his bed each morning. To Phil's horror she was brandishing his pyjama bottoms and he could see the streaks of dust across the seat. 'What *have* you been up to, young man?'

Her voice was no more than puzzled, and gently chiding – Aunt Luce enjoying the new experience of foster-parenthood.

Phil thought quickly. 'I – I had to get up in the night, and ... in the dark, I tripped on the landing.' Why hadn't he thought of wearing old trousers, as well as the anorak?

Aunt Luce sounded hurt. 'But I gave the landing a good brush only yesterday!'

Uncle Ern's blue eyes suddenly bored alarmingly into Phil's. 'What's wrong with the downstairs bathroom?'

'Pardon?'

'You heard. Why did you have to come upstairs?'

'I – I don't know . . . I was sleepy, and I didn't think.'

Aunt Luce waved the pyjamas, shrugging. 'Oh, well, they'll wash easy enough.'

Uncle Ern's gaze stayed speculatively on Phil and his fingers rustled against his unshaven chin.

'All set?' asked Andy.

Phil nodded. They left Andy's go-cart on the pavement at the front and walked as casually as they could through the short passage-way into the back garden. Taking hold of an end each, they carried the chest-of-drawers away and placed it carefully on the centre plank of the cart.

They both pushed, Andy awkwardly managing the steering ropes. They had turned the corner before Andy said, anxiously, 'He was watching from an upstairs window.'

'Who, Uncle Ern?'

'Unless it was Ebenezer's ghost.'

'Oh, crikey!'

'He can't have guessed what we're up to? Everything worked all right last night?'

'Like clockwork,' said Phil, but he felt uneasy.

7 Documents X

A bored young police constable at the crossroads opposite the telephone kiosk gave the odd vehicle and its burden a puzzled glance. The boys slowed as he raised his hand, then he suddenly grinned broadly and waved them on, pretending to be a traffic cop.

The Wasteland was deserted. At the Cave, breathless with having heaved the heavy load across the footbridges, they looked carefully to and fro, then Phil got busy with the padlock screws. Andy cleared enough of the rubbish heap to enable the door to open wider and they lifted the chest-of-drawers inside and closed the door behind them.

It was bitterly cold inside, but they were well wrapped up and Andy's candle provided an illusion of warmth. In turn they cupped their hands about the flickering flame before starting work.

Everything had remained dry and unharmed. For a while they scarcely spoke. They lifted out the contents of the drawers and laid them in rough order on the table. Books comprised the bulk; the fat, leather-bound volumes some of which Grandad had dropped that night. They bore long, complicated titles such as *Experiments and Practices in the Construction of Steam Engines*, and were by authors Phil had never heard of. One was printed in Latin, or so Andy said. They flicked through the pages of each book. The margins, in places, were heavily annotated in tiny, quite illegible handwriting long turned a misty brown, and there were many exquisite but equally incomprehensible little sketches: parts of mechanisms, doodlings, highly complex patterns of lines as though the reader – Ebenezer himself? – had been deep in thought.

Several small sheets of much-folded paper, crisp with age, slipped from between the tight pages. Phil carefully picked them up and, already at a loss, glanced at the meaningless scribblings, then put the sheets back.

Still silent, they gave their attention to three thinner, longer books in calf skin. On the otherwise empty endsheet of each, written in large, flowing figures, was a date – a year: 1842, 1843, 1844. The pages, torn and badly stained in places, were crammed with the close, unreadable handwriting already met with in the margins of the treatises on engineering. And more drawings ... parts of machinery, cogs, levers, cams and cut-away views of various cylindrical units. Phil, in an awed whisper, said, 'They're parts of an engine, I think. A locomotive.' Sadly, he was thinking of poor Grandad's lonely wakes over these long-dead inscriptions. They were diaries, of course, but could *anyone* ever make sense of such stuff?

'Look at this!' cried Andy. He had unrolled a large sheet of parchment which had been tied with faded ribbon. There was not room to spread it out properly, but they took a fascinated look at it near the candle.

The sheet contained further drawings, this time of a complete locomotive with detail work set apart in smaller assemblies. It was unlike anything Phil had seen before in books and museums, though he guessed that it belonged to a period later than George Stephenson's *Rocket*. Its boiler was longer, the fluted funnel shorter, and the chassis was sprung upon three sets of equal-sized wheels – what is called the 0–6–0 system. But at the rear was a strange, turreted structure, part of the cowling cut away to reveal a mass of intricate works.

Phil scowled at it. A new question was teasing his mind. Was this drawing the mere dream of a genius, a dream that had come to nothing outside Ebenezer's mad, twisted mind? Well, this drawing, and the others, would have fascinated

Grandad. But would they alone have spurred him on to that agitated, secretive search for a fortune – sent him climbing up into the attic night after night?

Certainly, here was Ebenezer's brain child – the child he had longed desperately to bring to birth in the forge. And now, as Phil awkwardly let the parchment crackle open further, he saw that the child had a name. It was printed in black ink, proudly beneath the plans:

STORMRIDER

Andy had drawn apart and was leafing through another of the thin books. This one had a tattered cardboard cover and was ruled on each page for accounts of money. 'What d'you make of this, Phil?'

They scanned the columns of figures – figures which were comparatively easy to read, but not the handwritten statements beside each amount. And not even these practical pages had been spared Ebenezer's incessant, restless scribblings.

Andy said, 'This one's got his name in it and the writing's the same. If all these amounts stand for the money Ebenezer saved up and hid away, there *must* be a fortune. Where would he have got it all?'

Phil said, 'He was an expert engineer. I expect he was well paid when he worked for George Stephenson up in Newcastle. And he probably invented a lot of small gadgets to do with locos.'

'Took out patents, you mean?' Trust Andy to know the right word! 'Yes, I see. And he'd go on getting money for them even after he came to Deptford. Royalties, I think they're called. Then he went crazy, and became a miser. . . .'

Phil's eyes widened with a fresh, sudden insight. 'Perhaps . . . perhaps he was saving up to build the *Stormrider*.'

'What, that old iron in the drawing?'

The expression annoyed Phil, but he let it pass. At that

moment a fast train roared along the viaduct, shaking the walls, thundering in their ears; it was the moment, perhaps, when Ebenezer turned over in his grave and the throbbing around them became his hollow laughter. . . .

Then the moment, like the train, hurtled by. Andy was saying, 'We haven't found the fortune yet, but this lot must be worth quite a bit. Museums, libraries – and there are railway societies, aren't there? Enthusiasts belong to them, and they'd buy some of this lot like a shot. . . .'

'I'm not selling it to them!'

'I know. I was only saying . . .'

Phil didn't listen. His fingers were plucking at the little brass fastenings of one of the flat, lizard skin cases which he'd left till the last. The shallow lid opened – and Phil gasped.

It was a photograph – a *sort* of photograph. It was elaborately framed in some kind of metal covered with gold-leaf. The craftsman who had made the frame had carved a surround of Greek columns, like the proscenium of a miniature theatre.

But it was no ordinary photograph; behind the small sheet of glass an image quivered – illusive, subtly shifting and changing depending upon the angle at which the case was held. There was a shimmering unreality, a coppery sheen to the picture, yet every little detail was starkly clear.

Phil saw the Benson house. Surely it *was* the Benson house? Yes, the gaunt, flat-fronted structure was unmistakable. Yet there were differences: some understandable, but others that were most puzzling.

There was a marked difference in setting. The house stood quite alone, there were no modern flats in the background, no lines of washing, no hint of squalor. Its brick walls and clean stone mouldings around the narrow windows looked fresh and untouched.

The other, stranger difference took some time for Phil to spot: *the house was shown the wrong way round*. In the real house the two tall windows of the big front parlour lay to the *left* of the door, from an observer's point of view. In the picture they were seen on the *right*.

The scene was very still, as though frozen in time. At one of the upstairs windows (Grandad's old living-room?) was a girl. The window was open, and she leaned forward with her hands grasping the sill. She had long, fair hair tied on each side with ribbons. She was smiling down at something happening, apparently, in the street.

Below, two other figures stood self-consciously beside the doorstep. One was a woman of middle age with bunched-back hair, bonnet, broad skirts and shawl. The second was a very old man with a long, bushy beard. He leaned slightly forwards on a stick and what could be seen of his face was wary and mildly amused.

At the edge of the picture – on the observer's right – a fourth figure was just visible, the blurred, ghostly image of a small boy playing with a hoop. It was as if he had intruded into the carefully composed picture from some different dimension: the effect was of several boys at play with several hoops.

Even Andy, coming to peer over Phil's shoulder, was silenced by these fresh mysteries. There were other photographs, each in its own little flat case. The second was more soberly framed in black wood and was similar in general appearance to the first; but now the girl had vanished from the upstairs window and come down to join the woman and the old man. On the right, the ghostly hoop no longer multiplied itself beside its hazy owner; this time the child appeared on the left, accompanied by a hazy dog. The dog could be recognized as a collie – or, rather, a number of collies superimposed upon each other in the same multi-dimensional way as the hoops in the first photograph.

Phil put this one down and opened the third case. Once more, there stood the Benson house reversed, with just a single figure taking up a Napoleonic posture – arm across his chest and one foot raised on the step. Apart from his different costume, top hat, cut-away jacket, narrow trousers and patterned waistcoat, he bore a striking resemblance to a younger, more fiery-eyed Grandad.

'Ebenezer!' Phil might have been uttering something holy. It was a guess, yet . . . who else could it be?

At last he laid down this photograph reverently with the others – and so came to the last of the cases. Beautifully framed, it showed an interior – the parlour of the Benson house? Yes, decided Phil, that would be so, but the heavy, dark furnishings were unimportant.

In the forefront, so that his seated form occupied almost the whole of the shimmering photo, was a boy. His arms rested on the sides of a tall-backed chair. His face was solemn, the eyes unnaturally large, the whole face thin and delicate – a sick face. He was dressed in stiff, Sabbath clothes, an unwilling captive of the photographer's art.

Andy laughed softly, eagerly: 'He's *you*!' he gasped. 'He's exactly like you.'

Phil nodded. He had just had the experience of gazing at his own face in a tiny mirror, a mirror that quivered and wavered, yet told no lie.

The candle flame burned low and began a sizzling death in the molten wax. Andy asked, 'Shall I light another?'

Phil didn't hear him. 'He's *Jamie*,' he said.

The candle went out and for a few moments, while Andy was groping for another, they were plunged into darkness.

A train roared frighteningly over their heads.

They spent a long time that day merely gazing at the pictures, wondering how they had been made and who had made them. The books and papers were set aside, while Phil, with Andy unusually silent at his elbow, identified the figures.

Here they were, the old, old Bensons. The bearded ancient was Stephen, Ebenezer's father. The woman with him could only be Sarah, the engineer's wife, and the fair-headed girl at the window was their daughter Elizabeth. The little boy playing first with the hoop and then with the collie was Timothy, who had grown up to marry Maggie the Tartar – and whose grandson was Phil's grandfather.

And Jamie, the sick one who had died so young after carving his initials on the viaduct wall. . . . He had a portrait to himself, granting those sad, dark eyes the power to gaze down through a tunnel of time, into the eyes of a descendant who so closely resembled him. . . .

They glanced through the diaries again, making nothing of the curious, alien script. In the end they were too tired and baffled and excited to pursue their investigations further, so they packed the precious documents into one of the packing cases far at the back of the Cave, hiding them carefully with the old, serge railway uniforms. Ebenezer's secrets would be safe there, if they were safe anywhere.

8 Who are the spies?

Several weeks went by, the days lengthening into February. At the house in Landmann Street, Uncle Ern's threatened changes took place. Mrs Partridge moved out to stay with her sister in Bermondsey and sometimes Phil called on her and brought her up to date with the news.

Uncle Ern set to work redecorating the ground floor, saying that he wanted to 'improve the property'. He might wish to sell the house, and he might not; he seemed to take a malicious pleasure in keeping Aunt Luce, and Phil, in suspense about his plans. Phil watched, and waited. He knew that Uncle Ern's activities were giving him ample opportunity for clearing out odd corners and prying, undisturbed, wherever he wished. Phil decided that his uncle must, by now, have made a search of the attic and in that case he must have found the trunk.

Had he opened it, discovering the old clothing? If so, since Phil had long ago flung the little brass key into the canal, he must have forced the lock and been disappointed. Phil hoped that would be the end of the matter, and Uncle Ern would think of no connection between that and Phil's excursion on the landing the night he'd removed Documents X.

Phil got his old bedroom back, so, although he did *not* listen at keyholes, he couldn't help overhearing a good deal of what his aunt and uncle said in their room. There were many arguments, and voices were frequently raised. Aunt Luce would vow that she wouldn't stay another week in 'this dreadful old house', but take Phil to Luton, with or without Uncle Ern. Uncle Ern would tell his wife to 'see reason', and 'be patient'. Once, Phil overheard more clearly the mysterious remark he'd related to Andy. . . . 'Look, that old tyke knew what he was talking about, or I wouldn't be wasting my time, would I?' Aunt Luce snorted, 'You've said yourself he was drunk. He was probably only spinning a yarn.'

Phil was sure they were referring to the person whom Uncle Ern had met in Luton, and whose information had led to the sending of that fatal postcard.

The boys went to the Cave as often as they could. They took the documents out of the packing case and sifted through them with chilled, stiff fingers. Ebenezer's astonishing script remained as impossible as ever, so they concentrated on the drawings, and the fascinating photographs. Often, for Phil, as the candle flame danced across the glass sheets and trains hurtled overhead, the figures in the pictures would seem, for a second, to come to life like actors on their tiny stage. Old Stephen's smile, was it more ironical and wise? Didn't Elizabeth dart her beautiful eyes at her brother, Timothy, at his ghostly play? And surely Ebenezer's stare burned quick with some strange hurt and appeal. . . . Phil, his imagination drenched with these startlingly real images, felt that at any moment the old Bensons would open their mouths and speak, and he would hear what they said.

And poor, sick Jamie . . . how easy it was to fancy that his pale, thin lips moved, their urgent message pitifully trapped behind the rectangle of glass.

Even after Phil had carefully replaced the fragile pictures in their lizard skin cases, the Bensons' faces went on living in his imagination.

But he did not tell Andy this.

One day a small bombshell dropped. At tea-time Aunt Luce was silent. She asked Phil none of her well-meaning questions about his day at school. The atmosphere was tense.

Uncle Ern stared moodily at his food, picked the shell of a hard-boiled egg to pieces, then gulped it down too quickly. Afterwards, his mouth still full of bread and butter, he pushed his chair aside and said, 'Come in the bedroom. I want a word with you.'

Grandad's metal trunk lay on the floor like a small, rusty coffin. Uncle Ern jerked his head at it. 'You wouldn't know where the key to that is, would you?'

His tone was flat and casual, but Phil sensed the impending menace behind it. 'Lost your tongue? I said, do you know where the key is?'

'Key?'

Uncle Ern finally emptied his mouth, then deftly rolled himself a cigarette. His cold, blue look came through the familiar smoke cloud. 'Quite a Little Sir Echo, aren't you? I say "key", then you say "key", and we get nowhere fast. This was the old man's trunk, wasn't it? And you know where he kept it, and maybe what used to be in it?'

Phil had met this trick of Uncle Ern's: the triple question, designed to confuse him. It was difficult to avoid nodding at least once. Phil managed to keep his head, and his tongue, still.

'Are you trying to tell me you've never been up in that attic, never seen this trunk?'

This time Phil was caught out. If only he'd said 'yes' at once, it wouldn't have mattered. There could have been no harm in merely admitting that he'd *seen* the trunk. As it was, Uncle Ern rightly interpreted Phil's hesitation as a desire to conceal some important truth about it.

Like a good conjuror, Uncle Ern was never short of tricks. Suddenly, with a skilful flick of his toe, he kicked the lid of the trunk open, exposing the useless rags beneath.

So he had already forced the lock. He hadn't needed a key.

'Now, I wonder why the old man would keep a trunk, full of old rags, locked up in the attic? Or ...' He watched Phil closely. 'Or did it used to hold something more interesting?'

Phil remained sullen and uncommunicative. Uncle Ern clenched his fists threateningly – Phil half expected a swipe. 'All right, you crafty little beggar. I'll get at the truth, sooner or later.'

Phil wondered if Uncle Ern knew even more than his manner suggested: Phil's visit to the upstairs bathroom, the dusty pyjamas, the removal, seen from a window, of the chest-of-drawers the following morning.

And the fear gripped him ... how long would it be before Uncle Ern's grasping curiosity reached out as far as the viaduct?

One Sunday morning Phil lay in bed looking at the print of the viaduct on his wall. The picture must, he thought at first, portray the scene as it had been on a Sunday. It was so serene, so still. The feathery trees were like plumes on best hats.

Then he remembered that it could not have been a Sunday, because of the train. At that time, trains had run only on weekdays. On Sundays, people had walked along the railway tracks, admiring the view of old London. At night, Grandad had told him, gas lamps had been strung along the parapets in golden chains.

The stretch of the viaduct in the picture passed through Bermondsey, nearer London Bridge than Deptford. The arch where he had found the Cave, the other upon which Jamie Benson had carved his initials, these were not shown. Neither was there any trace of engine workshops. Yet, as early as that, such shops had existed, somewhere.

Had Jamie carved the inscription to pass the time whilst

waiting for Ebenezer to come away from his work in the shops? Several different locomotives, some of them forgotten even by railway historians, had trundled up and down that primitive line. The engines had been hauled up steep ramps and Grandad had shown Phil changes in the brickwork marking where the ramps had been.

Phil thought of the old photographs. They at least, surely, had been taken on a Sunday? Ebenezer's top hat, Elizabeth's silky dress ... not exactly garments put on every day by a family kept hungry and impoverished by a miserly, crazy genius.

But would they have let young Timothy bowl his hoop on the Sabbath?

Phil yawned, got out of bed, and dressed. Through his window the February day was raw and sunless. A few bits of washing hung, limp and dead, on the lines across the flat roofs. While he was buttoning his shirt he had the feeling which came so often nowadays – that the mystery was other than it seemed; something more, something ... different?

'Where's Uncle Ern, Auntie?'

'I haven't the least idea.' The bitter little lines at her mouth corners twitched. 'He's always off somewhere; "seeing a man about a certain prospect", "clinching a spot of business, my girl", "having a chat with a bloke who can put us on to a good thing".'

Phil looked at her, smiling. The kitchenette seemed much more friendly with just the two of them. 'Has Uncle Ern always been like that? I mean, wanting lots of money and thinking he can get it easily?'

Aunt Luce put a lump of fat into the frying pan, but her eyes were fixed ahead, as though in the direction of a faraway youth. 'Yes, it's a sort of disease. When we were first married we were going to run a boarding house at Margate,

and retire on the proceeds after ten years. Then it was junk – "war surplus", it was called. He got in with an old schoolmate of his here in Deptford, and the two of them started a yard. Ernie's partner was dishonest – I don't think Ernie was – and they got a bad name between them. We left the district – in a hurry.'

'Where did you go?'

'That first time? Oh, all over. It was a taxi business in Birmingham. Then it was a greengrocer's in Chatham. After that, he got this job as a bus conductor in Luton, then he and a couple of cronies started the second-hand car business. The bottom fell out of that a few months ago. They had to sell it for a song.'

'But he told me he'd struck lucky in business, and bought the bungalow. . . .'

Aunt Luce laughed. 'Well, you *could* put it like that. The bungalow isn't much – though I like it there. We still owe most of the money. Now it looks as if, once the legal side's settled, we'll stay here and pick up the threads. I don't really mind, now. I've got used to the trains, and I will say Ernie's making an effort to spruce the place up . . . besides, there's you to consider. . . .'

'Auntie, do you *hate* Uncle Ern?'

Aunt Luce looked startled. 'Hate him? Of course not . . . what a question! Anyway, it isn't as simple as that. You'll understand when you're older. The funny thing is, your Uncle Ern's like all you Bensons. In his own queer, aggravating way he's a dreamer . . . and his dreams never come true. It's like that with this stupid "nest egg" business . . .' She gave Phil a strange look as she switched off the gas. 'You know, he still thinks you know where it is – or something about it.'

It wasn't quite a question, and she didn't pursue it. While his aunt was serving the eggs and bacon, Phil was thinking about what she'd said, and how true it was when you stopped to think. . . . Uncle Ern being a dreamer, and disappointed and angry because his yearnings were always thwarted. 'Like all you Bensons . . .' Even, in a way, like Ebenezer himself?

Daringly, breaking a long silence, Phil said, 'Aunt Luce – swap you secrets?'

'What's that?' Another sharp look, as if she half guessed what was coming. 'Well, I don't know.'

'I promise not to tell, then *you* promise. But you tell me something first.'

'That sounds like one of your Uncle Ern's bargains!' laughed Aunt Luce. 'Go on, try me.'

'Why did Uncle Ern come here in the first place, and who's the "old tyke" who found out about Grandad's secret?'

'That's two questions. And some crafty young man's been listening at keyholes!'

'I didn't . . .'

'All right, I'll tell you, for what it's worth. Your grandad used to keep lodgers. One of them was an old layabout by the name of Paddy O'Reilly – a real Irish yarn-spinner if ever there was one . . . you don't remember him?'

Phil shook his head. There had been so many lodgers.

'Well, it was years after we left here. Anyway, your uncle happened to come across this O'Reilly in a pub up Luton way. It was one of those queer chances. . . . To cut a long story short, this lodger said that while he was here your grandad got him to do some odd jobs about the place. He'd asked him to look out for any hollow places in the walls downstairs, loose floorboards and the like. According to this O'Reilly, your grandad was always prodding about, even digging up part of the garden, searching for what he called "family heirlooms".'

'And Uncle Ern believed him, sent the postcard. . . .'

'Yes, and of course he'd heard all the usual family talk

81

since he was a boy. After his gossip with the Irishman, washed down with a good few pints I dare say, your uncle decided that his father might have found money, and be keeping quiet about it. It became – what's it called? – an obsession with him. In the end, he made up his mind to come here and bully the truth out of your grandad. That's about it. Do you want any more to eat?'

'No, thanks . . . well, there *was* something, Auntie. But not money. Least, we haven't found it yet. . . .'

Phil told Aunt Luce, then, about the trunk, Grandad's fatal efforts to get it down from the attic that day when the postcard had arrived, and the means Phil and Andy had used to smuggle out the documents. The only thing he did not tell was where they were. He could not bring himself to betray the whereabouts of the Cave, even to a confidant under oath. Aunt Luce did not ask.

'Your Uncle Ern's guessed a lot of that, as you know,' she said, quietly. 'So, for that matter, did I – but I don't reckon it's any of my business. You Bensons must just sort it all out for yourselves.'

'But you're one of us, Aunt Luce. What do you think we ought to do?'

'I think you and I had better sit tight on our secrets! And watch out for your Uncle Ern. He's still on the war-path, and getting warmer, so to speak.'

Phil grinned. 'You're all right, Aunt Luce. . . .' Then he added, thoughtlessly impetuous. 'Grandad was wrong about one thing – he called you flighty!'

Aunt Luce looked hurt; then she smiled wearily. 'Well, maybe I was on the flighty side when I was younger. He'd think so, anyway. But it's funny . . . I liked your grandad, Phil. I respected him. He was one of the old school – straight and good, for all his funny Benson ways. . . .'

Phil hastened to make amends. 'He would have liked you, too, Aunt Luce – now.'

Understanding a little about Uncle Ern did not make him easier to like. He ambled in from a Sunday morning walk, rolled his inevitable cigarette and put on his staring act. 'Tell us about this camp of yours.'

'Camp?'

'Don't come the Sir Echo again. You told us you had a camp. Isn't that where you spend most of your time, with that mate of yours . . . what'sisname . . .?'

'Andy – Andy Smith.'

'That's the one. And you've got a camp.'

'Sort of. It's only a game. . . .'

'Where?'

'Where?'

'You heard! Over in that wasteground near the viaduct?'

Phil's heart jumped. Despite Aunt Luce's warning, he hadn't expected Uncle Ern to have got *that* warm.

'We used to muck about in them arches, when we was kids,' said Uncle Ern, musingly, staringly. 'Your dad and me got a belting from the old man, once, for getting ourselves smothered in tar from some old barrel. The tar was stored in one of them arches. We busted the door in. Least, I did. Your dad was on the timid side, but he still got his share of the good hiding.' Uncle Ern grinned, relishing the injustice of it. 'So you aren't telling us where your camp is – right? Never mind. I've got ways of finding out, if I want to. If you're up to something in them arches, I'll get to know soon enough.'

'Just up there,' said Phil, that afternoon, 'the trains stopped while tickets were collected. And while that happened crowds of urchins would shout up to the passengers, "Throw down your mouldy coppers." And sometimes they did.'

Andy kicked idly at the weedy path edging. His toe

excavated an old locomotive buffer spring which he sent dancing off into the undergrowth.

'Don't suppose we'll find any pennies still lying about now.'

'Not far from here, somewhere, they built a specimen house right under the arches. I've seen a picture. The idea was that people would live in houses under the arches, and the rents they paid would help pay for the railway. It didn't work though. People couldn't stand the noise of the trains, and water leaked through from the track.'

Andy grinned. 'You don't pay much rent for *your* arch, do you?'

Phil grinned back, feeling for his penknife.

Inside the Cave, before they took Documents X from their hiding place, Phil told Andy what Aunt Luce had said about the past lodger, Paddy O'Reilly.

'So that's how it was?' Andy gave Phil a sharp look. 'You didn't say anything about the trunk?'

Phil skilfully avoided a direct lie. 'As if I'd let Uncle Ern know anything!'

It was always difficult trying to explain Aunt Luce to Andy. Andy wouldn't accept that she could be different from Uncle Ern. To Andy, both Bensons were the Enemy, indivisible. He liked his characters plain and straightforward: they were either good or bad, friends or foes, like the cowboys in comics who wore white hats or black.

In case Andy should see through the deception, Phil hurried on to tell him what Uncle Ern had asked. Andy whistled. 'You know what that means, don't you? He's got *spies* planted out here. He's having us watched.'

'You really think so?' Put in such dramatic terms, the thought sounded frightening. But Andy seemed to be half-enjoying the prospect.

He nodded slowly in the candlelight. 'From now on, chum, we've got to watch our step, make sure we aren't being shadowed when we come here, and look out for busy-bodies.'

And sooner or later, Phil thought, as they renewed their mostly futile study of Ebenezer's documents, they'd have to seek help in their quest. There must be someone who could read the diaries, establish once and for all whether the story of the hidden fortune were true or false – someone they could trust.

Yet there was no hurry, so long as the papers stayed hidden; so long as Uncle Ern, and Andy's sinister spies, were kept at bay . . .

Phil smiled to himself, realizing that now *he* was thinking like a character in a comic. Perhaps, one day soon, they could contact Dan Dare, or Batman, or whoever was available at the time. And along they'd come with death rays, fleets of rockets, vanquishing the Wicked Uncle Ern and his Minions and leading them into some real, deep cavern a-glitter with long-buried golden sovereigns . . .

'Pardon?'

'I said, there've been a lot of kids about, lately. We haven't seen many other kids all winter. Now they're crawling out from under stones, like hibernating insects. We'd better watch them, Phil. Your Uncle Ern may have got *kids* to spy on us. Some of them would do anything for sixpence. . . .'

Whatever his plans for the viaduct, Uncle Ern was clearly not relinquishing his hope of finding something in the house in Landmann Street. By now every corner must have been swept clean, tapped, floorboards raised and nailed back; torch beams fed into inaccessible places, lino lifted, loose bricks removed and remortared. A wretched time for spiders, ants and silver-fish and, perhaps, for Uncle Ern, whose moodiness increased with the passing days.

Over in the Wasteland, Andy glared just as moodily at

anybody who dared poke an unfamiliar head anywhere near the Cave. The boys were more aware of the bustle and clangour of the arch workshops, the comings and goings of vans, cars and trucks.

One day, they came face to face with a tramp in one of the derelict streets near the railway. He'd apparently slept the night in one of the boarded-up terraced cottages due for demolition. He wore filthy clothes, a black, matted beard and a cap which might have been borrowed from a scarecrow. He eyed the boys warily then, for some strange reason of his own, shuffled after them some way along the street. At first, Andy was certain *he* was a spy – but they never saw him again.

But several times they spotted a small, bent figure with white hair stuffed like feathers beneath a shapeless hat. He seemed to be forever examining the brickwork of the viaduct arches, looking up at the parapets, poking about among the junk heaps with a walking stick. Sometimes he would take a small notebook from his pocket and jot something down with a stub of pencil. His lips could be seen to move, his head shake. Once he tried the locked door of an arch not far from the Cave. Andy insisted upon following him: each current suspect received this furtive treatment, but they lost him somewhere amidst the criss-cross complexity of streets.

Then ... there was the girl. A tall, fair girl of about their own age whom they did not recognize. Perhaps she lived on the other side of the viaduct and attended a different school.

On Saturdays and Sundays she was invariably accompanied by a horde of shouting kids, mostly much younger than herself. They chased and squealed over the waste ground, clattering in the junk heaps. Sometimes their activity would attract the persecution of another set of children – bigger, hostile boys who threw sticks and stones and flung jeers and taunts. The girl would fight back with venom and hatred, like a slender, graceful snake guarding her brood.

Once she and Andy came face to face and a stony, unfriendly look passed between them, but no word.

Sometimes the girl and her brood would vanish – vanish completely like the Pied Piper and the Hamelin children into the mountain. Where they went, and what they did, worried Andy.

He preferred to have his suspect spies in full view.

9 The secret garden

Spring was coming early to the Wasteland. The coarse, tough grass resumed its growth against the old brick arches of the viaduct. Here and there the ground between the junk heaps was speckled with colour. New weeds slipped eager, pale tendrils from beneath the rotting tyres of abandoned vehicles; brambles and bindweed began to crochet patterns in the chain-link fencing around the factory. The bits of broken bottles were jagged eyes winking in new sunlight.

Vagrant birds experimented with nests under the high parapets – nests that would soon tremble to pieces with the constant throb of train wheels. Heavy pigeons flapped their wings and, like shabby old tramps, sought a greener hospitality in parks and squares.

It was at about this time that Molly Perkins found the garden. Not far out of Deptford centre, a street wandered diagonally in the direction of the canal. Part of the Wasteland, in fact, was formed by the triangle between this street and the railway. An alley full of tin sheds, rubbish heaps and lock-up garages cut part-way through the triangle. At the end of the alley was Eccles's junk yard. Then, for the rest of the space, the gardens of the houses stretched narrow and long until they ran out of room, coming up against the embankment of a section of the District Line, along which scurried the red trains of London Transport.

The house at the end of the street possessed the thinnest, longest garden of all. It came to a rather indefinite end at a broken barbed-wire fence right in the middle of a small jungle of stunted trees and bushes. It was the indefiniteness, plus the sniffling coaxing of one of Molly's younger brothers, that eventually led her to put one long leg experimentally over the wire, getting quite a nasty scratch in the process, and, after a fruitless glimpse into the jungle, to draw the second leg after the first.

Molly was well aware that they were trespassing. The fence told her that. And in case the fence lied, a trellis full of straggly rose leaves, a strip of whiskery lawn and the distant glimpse of a grey rooftop made the fact certain. On the other hand, the young brother had stopped sniffling, the trellis provided an almost peep-proof screen and Molly could see no possible objection to their scouting around.

Besides, it was quite likely the house was empty – perhaps even in the course of being demolished. Of course, that *must* be it! Nobody who owned a garden could possibly let it turn into such a wilderness as this. Molly and her five younger brothers and sisters lived in a flat, and flats do not normally have gardens.

It was not long before the place became a favourite playground for Molly and what people smilingly referred to as her 'gang'. It was a garden of delights; almost a *secret* garden – except, of course, that when you have five brothers and sisters, real secrets are hard to come by, and even harder to keep. And as well as the brothers and sisters, there were the neighbours' children, their dolls, sometimes their pets and toys, all to be kept amused, comforted and cared for. 'She's such a good little mother' the neighbours said, as though (Molly decided during her occasional resentful moods) she were a character in a Victorian story book. They meant it was useful, while they were out shopping or busy about the house, to have someone who was good at blowing noses, drying tears and patching cut knees, to look after their offspring.

Molly, who had once glanced through a book about bird watching, called the garden their 'hide'. A hide it was, for there was quite a lot to hide *from*.

The Viaduct

Those big boys, for instance. It was hard for Molly to
explain what she hoped was true: that the big boys did
not mean any harm. They simply liked playing wars, and
Indians, and Thunderbirds. Having no other imaginary
enemies in sight, they were liable to pick on Molly and her
gang. They shouted things. They whooped and jeered.
They threw things, missiles, they called them.

The big boys always seemed to emerge from the direction of the Eccles's junk yard. Old Eccles, a grinning,
oafish creature, behaved like a big, oafish, middle-aged boy
himself, the way he seemed to egg them on. Then, when a
quite nasty skirmish broke out, with Molly losing her
temper and flinging back the missiles and the taunts as
fast as they arrived, he would go chortling off in to the tin
hut he called his office and dissociate himself from any
serious trouble that might develop.

There were other things to escape from, rain, for instance, and right at the end of the garden was a disused
shed where they could huddle and listen to Molly's creepy
stories, shrinking delightedly as she whispered of witches
and ghosts. The garden was a haven from the bricked-in
dullness of the streets. It was green, and half-wild flowers
were beginning to thread zig-zag necklaces of colour
around the lawn, which grew longer every day. It was
almost like being in a park. There was even an old wooden
swing with one post that jerked to and fro when the
smaller children were perched precariously on the broken
seat: thonk, thunk; thonk; thunk . . .

Best of all, there was the piano, a very ancient instrument
abandoned there on its front so long ago that the keyboard,
if it still possessed one, was buried in the soft earth of a
rubbish heap. But you could still play some of the exposed,
rusty strings – banging them with sticks, or plucking with
a piece of metal. Molly, who was musical, got all kinds of

tunes out of it and forbade any of the younger children to touch it.

Sooner or later, of course, the big boys would find the garden. There was also, one day, an ominous thread of smoke from the chimney of the house: like a finger of doom, or a warring redskin's smoke signal. At first, Molly tapped extra gently on the piano strings, lest one of her ragged little tunes should bring a new enemy upon them. Then, with a sort of fatalism, she stopped caring. Suppose whoever lived in the house *did* find them? What harm were they doing? Anyway, it was fun while it lasted.

Unaware that she had already been marked down by Andy Smith as Spy Number Two (Number One was the bent old eccentric they had seen mumbling about among the viaduct arches), Molly Perkins noticed the two *other* boys as they made their various excursions along the path. One was ginger haired and one was dark, and they both strolled along as though they had all day. They didn't jeer. They didn't throw 'missiles'. All she got from either of them were cold, suspicious stares.

'Snooty pair! I wonder what they're up to?' she thought, as she stared back. Contrarily, she despised them because they were not rough and rude like the Eccles boys.

It was the shifty manner in which Andy walked and the way he kept glancing back over his shoulder, that eventually roused her curiosity, made her wonder what exactly drew them so regularly along the viaduct. Where did they go? It was none of Molly Perkins' business, but that didn't stop her wondering.

'She's watching us, now,' said Andy.

'She won't see much,' said Phil. He was a little tired of Andy's role as spy-catcher. In any case, this Saturday they were not going straight to the cave. A little farther along they would cut up a street into Deptford and visit the

churchyard. Phil had never actually shown Andy the
Benson grave, and Andy had asked to see it. He wanted
to read the names and dates on the tombstone for himself.

Phil had not been here since that winter's day when
Grandad had taken him. Now it all looked different. Bright
sunlight shone on newly planted flowers and shrubs in
freshly turned earth. Someone had pruned back the ivy
from the blackened stone. Unmoving, as though through
the whole of time, the angel ignored them, reserving his
gentle smile for those over whom, symbolically, he watched.
His wings were splendid and white in the sunshine.

Andy's lips moved down the names, as Grandad's had
done. He even bent down to move a stem of ivy which had
concealed the last name – that of 'Maggie the Tartar'. He
was about to ask some question when a voice said, close
beside them, 'Excuse me, do you mind if I take a peep,
too?'

Very puzzled, Mr Horace Felix watched the two boys
scamper off through the churchyard gate. Quite unaware,
of course, that Andy Smith had long ago designated him
Suspect Spy Number One, he wondered why his inoffen-
sive intervention at the graveside should have had such
startling results.

For a frantic moment Mr Felix even wondered whether
his pocket had been picked. He was anxiously feeling for
his wallet when he remembered that small boys rarely
picked pockets, except in the pages of *Oliver Twist*. Neither
of those boys had looked in the least like the Artful Dodger.
As soon as Mr Felix had spoken they had simply hopped
off, like a pair of shy, frightened sparrows.

Mr Felix shook his head, adjusted his spectacles, and
stooped to carry out his delayed inspection of the grave-
stone. He jotted down the inscriptions in his notebook,
nodded benignly at the angel, and shuffled away, deep in
thought.

His unhurried footsteps took him through the tangle of streets, along a stretch of the viaduct where he sometimes paused and peered myopically at some peculiarity of construction, then on to his house – the last of a terrace in Arum Street.

He turned the key in his front door. A very elderly, one-eyed cat greeted him inside with a plaintive miaow. 'Hello, Trevithick,' said Mr Felix.

He hung his hat and coat on a peg, exchanged shoes for slippers, put on his cosy, knitted smoking jacket, then went into the small parlour to poke the fire. As he entered the tiny kitchen to potter about getting his and Trevithick's lunch, he was thinking how fortunate he had been, a few weeks ago, to have been given the opportunity of purchasing such a snug little house. A widower for many years, with a grown-up family scattered round the world, Mr Felix had recently retired from a branch of the Railway Design Office, where he had worked for many years as a draughtsman. For a long time he and Trevithick had been bundled about from lodging to lodging, in which a succession of unfriendly landladies had taken a sudden dislike to poor Trevithick, because of his one eye, or to Mr Felix himself because of his untidiness and his habit of sitting up half the night burning extra electricity.

Mr Felix was an enthusiast – a railway enthusiast. Now that he had his own house again he could sit up reading and writing as late as he liked. What Mr Felix was mostly engaged upon at present was the book he had always planned to write 'when I have the time' – a book about London's railways.

Like most enthusiasts, Mr Felix had soon found that his hobby grew and grew like a beanstalk, with branches shooting out at all sorts of unexpected angles and with great fertility. He had not, at the start, intended to become interested in an obscure, eccentric inventor called Ebenezer

The Viaduct

Benson. The name had turned up, quite by accident, in some old letters Mr Felix had read in a museum. Now, Ebenezer and his doings were claiming more and more of his time, and keeping him up later and later at night.

On this Saturday after lunch, however, there was something different which had lain for several weeks on the old man's conscience. That garden! He had a house, and a man who owned a house ought to *care* about the garden that went with it. Mr Felix didn't exactly not care: he had just been so busy with other things. Now, when he opened the squeaky back door to let Trevithick out, the sun's rays came warmly and accusingly across the wilderness in front of the step. Gracious, thought Mr Felix. Apart from a cursory glance round when he had first moved in, he had never once set foot beyond the trellis!

He left the door open, got his pipe going nicely, then, hands in trouser pockets and still wearing his slippers, the enthusiast wandered up the long, thin slope towards the viaduct. And he had got almost as far as the trellis when he heard the strangest sounds imaginable.

Mr Felix did not believe in fairies, and he only *half* believed in angels. Yet ... wasn't that a harp he could hear? And voices ... a singing voice, rather pretty: a chuckling voice, and a less distinct, more sniffly sound that could just have been human. Mr Felix carefully parted the prickly stems of the climbing roses, looked mildly astonished, removed the pipe from his mouth and said, 'Hello! Where did you spring from?'

Molly Perkins looked up. The latest pop tune she was picking out on the old piano strings ended in a plaintive crescendo. Her first impulse was to run for it. But she had one of her younger brothers, a younger sister and one of the neighbour's semi-infants with her, and they couldn't run as fast as Molly. Molly stayed where she was and tried a smile. 'Hello! Is this your garden?'

'That's right.'

'Oh . . . I suppose we shouldn't really be here.'

'Strictly speaking, I suppose – no!'

Molly stared back, warily. The younger children watched Molly to see how she looked. 'And – you don't mind?'

'I haven't had time to think about it. I don't think so.'

Molly allowed her breath to escape. 'It's funny, I dreamt about you last night. Well, not exactly *you*. But I dreamt that the owner of that house – you do live there, don't you? – the owner came up and found us. He was a big, horrid man like old Eccles the junk man, and he chased us out with a stick.'

'And what did *you* do?'

'Woke up.' Then Molly, who felt the conversation ought to be made to go on, asked, 'Do you have dreams sometimes?'

'Oh, yes – I do,' and Mr Felix looked quite dreamy as he said this. He sat on an upturned box, relit his pipe and nodded at the piano. 'You get quite a tune out of that. Until I get to know your name, do you mind if I call you Madame Beethoven?'

'It's Molly Perkins. Who's Madame Beethoven?'

'Never mind her! Blow that young fellow's nose, then tell me what you were saying about dreams.'

10 The first of the dreams

It was that night that Phil had the first of his strange dreams. He was standing, quite alone, in the Cave; but there were no shelves or packing cases, nothing save a great, hollow emptiness. He seemed to be waiting in front of an arch filled in with bricks. It was the height of a door, with a curved lintel, and he knew, in his dreams, that if it was a door, and it opened, he would be able to walk through into the arch-room beyond.

There was no table, no candle sizzling in its wax-filled tin lid – yet there *was* light. Strangely, the light came from a train thundering overhead. The train was extraordinarily long, seeming to throb on and on for ever. The bogeys jumped, set after set, and Phil had a notion that it was a circular train. Somehow it was racing round and round a ringed track and, by some miracle that did not seem important, the lights from the unseen carriages shed their jerky, flickering rays through solid brickwork, making patterns on the walls like latticed screens.

Phil had the feeling that if he troubled to look upwards, he would see into the carriages – the people inside reading their newspapers or glancing out of dusty windows or dozing their unending journey through.

This seemed to go on for time immeasurable, then, with no particular surprise, Phil saw the brick arch open away from him. It made no sound. For a moment there was only blackness beyond, but suddenly a face, made luminous and criss-crossed by flickers, formed itself slowly, then there appeared the complete figure of a girl.

Phil recognized her at once – the pensive smile, the gold,

beribboned hair, the full-skirted dress. It was the girl from the old photographs, Elizabeth Benson.

Did she beckon? Before Phil was sure, the dream changed like the abrupt switching of slides in a magic lantern. The train was still rattling crazily round and round, but the chatter of its wheels was drawing away. And the light had gone, too: there was no seeing, only *feeling*, a sense that he was in a dark, narrow place. But he was not alone . . . someone else was close . . . ahead of him. They were in a tunnel, and even dream tunnels stayed dark.

There was the smell of old, dusty timber. On some impulse Phil got down on his knees, found himself crawling, like a very small child, along a floor dusty and prickly with splinters.

The space about him shrank, smaller and smaller, until even the little scraping sounds of his hands and knees, the quick panting of his lungs, were close and big and important. Phil was suddenly afraid – anxious and fretful, as if he were shut up in a stifling box and couldn't open the lid. Then, quite suddenly, fresh light – and air – burst upon him.

There was another image-switch as if a transparent slide had been changed. He was sitting, squeezed up, at a different opening. On the other side the girl sat, smiling, waiting . . . Her lips moved, but Phil could not hear what she said. The sound of the train was still in his ears, and Elizabeth's mouth was a meaningless changing of shapes. But her look was teasing, as though she were telling him what a slowcoach he was, he *still* hadn't caught her.

Phil crawled on through and crouched beside her. They were in a kitchen of some sort. A scullery? Unquestionably it was a place for cooking, hanging up of pots, drying of cloths, washing of clothes. Looming over them was a huge, stone copper – they had crawled from behind it, and Elizabeth in her Sabbath finery, too! The copper had a thick, wooden lid. Across the cold, stone floor stood a mangle with wide, ugly-toothed black-iron cogwheels and wooden rollers as broad as drums. A massive stove glowed red with hot coals.

Everything was plain and heavy: big chunks and blobs of wood, stone and metal. The room was full of steam.

The next image-switch was one of sound ... voices, muffled and distorted, replacing the throbbing of the train. And other sounds came ... the slam of a door, the bark of a dog. A woman was bent over a thick, scrubbed table cutting up vegetables with a long, broad knife. She turned, looked at them, and spoke; Phil caught the rise and fall of cadence, but could not quite grasp what she said. The words would not join intelligibly together. But she smiled at Phil, very compassionately, as if with recognition, rather than surprise at his appearance.

A small boy rushed in, bowling a hoop; rushing, rushing as little children will into dangerous places full of heat and sharpness. The dog, a collie, barked again and entered in pursuit of the small boy, its coarse coat brushing against Phil's knees. Boy and dog passed out of sight. The woman called after them, her face briefly exasperated and stern.

Another door slammed. Elizabeth touched Phil's arm and then, with a teasing smile over her shoulder, ran with a girl's daintiness into the next room. Phil followed, and found himself in a place that, in size and shape, was familiar from some half-forgotten encounter. The furniture, the heavy curtains hanging at two tall windows ... they, too, were only partly strange. On the big mantel-shelf over the fireplace stood several tall, fat candles, cold in brass holders, like the candles on an altar.

Daylight crept in at the windows. On the other side of the glass, the scene was startlingly bright and still. Nothing stood to overshadow the broad and spacious scene ... except the viaduct. Out there the feathery elms did not stir, and a short, squat train was frozen still above the elegant arches.

A very old man nodded from a rocking chair beside the fireplace. His stare was bright and friendly and, in the midst of his Santa Claus whiskers, thin lips parted in a spoken greeting. Suddenly he turned his head, changed the focus of his gaze, and looked at something, or someone, behind Phil. Phil spun round. In the same instant, a hand rested on his shoulder, and when he glanced up he saw Ebenezer Benson smiling at him. This was the Ebenezer of the old photograph, wearing cravat, cut-away jacket and top hat.

Elizabeth had gone to greet him, but his gaze was for Phil alone. It was the tender, caring, recognizing look that Sarah Benson had given him in the scullery, before turning to scold the boisterous little Timothy and his dog.

But Ebenezer's eyes had no part of the smile, for they burned with an agony that even the vivid portrait had not revealed. They were tortured, unhappy eyes . . .

Phil did not remember the whole of this dream at once. During the next day, bits of it came back to him at separate times, like doors opening into memories.

It was useless telling himself that dreams should never be taken too seriously, morbidly dwelt upon. To him this dream had a strange, compelling substance of its own. It had happened, and its memory belonged to him, to his experience and learning, as much as any real happening. There was some detail that bothered Phil beyond all the others. Was it something the dream had shown him? Something especially odd about the Bensons he had 'met'? No, they had scarcely come alive as real people, except in so far as weeks of gazing at their candle-lit features had lent them a kind of life in Phil's imagination. Then, what was the detail?

Suddenly Phil remembered. He had, so to speak, been

introduced, in the dream, to all the Bensons of the photographs save one.

He had not 'met' Jamie.

On Sunday afternoon, when he met Andy at the Cave, Phil did not mention the dream. Andy, in any case, was full of a fresh scandal: he had actually seen Suspect Spy Number One in deep and ominous conversation with Suspect Spy Number Two! All that had happened, in fact, was that Mr Felix, quite by chance, had met Molly and some of her charges along the viaduct path and the two had resumed the cheerful acquaintance struck up in the garden the day before. They had all jogged along together for a little way, before parting. None of them had seen Andy and Phil because Andy had insisted on their both being concealed inside an arch as they passed. But later Molly did catch a glimpse of them, and again came the teasing curiosity about where they went, and why. . . .

Phil, even more wrapped up in his own thoughts than usual, heard some of what Andy was saying, but not much.

'Well, what are we going to do about them?' demanded Andy.

'About them?'

'No wonder Uncle Ern calls you "Little Sir Echo"!'

'Oh, *them*! Well, I don't think they're spying on us. They don't *look* like spies.'

Andy winced disgustedly. 'Don't be such a twerp! Spies never look like spies. That's why they *are* spies. We both know that Uncle Ern's got somebody to watch us, right?'

'Well, we guessed.'

'And that funny little old boy like some character out of Charles Dickens. . . .'

'Pickwick.'

'Pickwick . . . he was hanging round the grave, wasn't he?'

'Yes, but . . .' Phil couldn't see why spies who had been specially selected because they didn't look what they were, should present themselves in such obvious attitudes of espionage. He was also tempted to remind Andy that it had been he who had grabbed Phil's arm the previous day and dragged him off in confusion, when it might have been more sensible either to stay and discover what else the little man had to say, or discreetly follow him and find out where he lived.

But Andy said, 'What exactly are you looking for?'

Phil removed a couple of the packing cases from a position midway along one curved wall and peered beyond. 'There's a small arch behind these shelves.'

'Well, all the arches have them, don't they?'

'Yes. I was just making sure.'

'Why?' Andy was interested, ready to embrace any new possibility, any fresh approach to the riddle that had so stubbornly eluded them. 'You're not thinking Ebenezer might have hidden his money out here, somewhere in the viaduct?'

Phil didn't answer. He was staring at the cold, blank bricks, the recessed arch which was identical with that in his dream. This, he realized, meant little or nothing. All the arches they had ever looked into had them. There was no reason why the Cave should be an exception.

Andy persisted, 'Where did you say Ebenezer's workshops used to be?'

Phil shook his head. 'I don't think Grandad was sure.'

'I wonder what's inside the arches on each side of us. . . .'

They had thought about this before. Since the neighbouring arches were both more securely, and more recently, padlocked than the Cave, they had assumed that some official or business concern had rented them for storage space. There was no way of finding out, short of bursting open the doors, or drilling through the walls.

Phil replaced the packing cases. Andy was already opening the one containing Documents X. He had grown tired of the old photographs, but the drawings fascinated him. They had both spent hours going through books about locomotives which they borrowed from the public library, trying to trace an engine resembling Ebenezer's plans. They found none quite like it.

The candle suddenly went into convulsions. A draught had entered the Cave, accompanied by a sliver of light beneath the door.

The boys swivelled round. Very slowly the door was being eased ajar. Andy strode forward, grabbed the edge and pushed. Taken unawares, the intruder on the other side was practically knocked off her feet.

Molly Perkins!

'You're hurting my arm!'

Mercilessly, Andy pulled her inside and slammed the door shut. His eyes blazed with triumph at Phil. 'Who said she wasn't a spy?' He gave the arm a wrench. 'All right – tell us how much he's paying you? What's he promised you for giving away where this place is?'

'I don't know what you're talking about!' The girl's face was white in the candle flame. 'I – I just wanted to know where you went.'

Andy let go of her arm, but stood between her and the door. 'Oh, yes? Then how come you're working with that other nosy character? The old man with a bent hat – Pickwick. . . .'

'Pickwick?' Molly's frightened face suddenly burst into smiles. The transformation was astonishing. Still rubbing her arm, she said, 'He'd laugh if he knew you called him that. His real name's Mr Felix. He's kind, and nice. He writes books, I think . . . and he didn't mind when he found us playing at the top of his garden. . . .'

'Us? Who's *us*?'

'The kids I look after. . . .'

Andy made for the door again. 'You didn't bring *them* with you?'

'Oh, have some sense! I'm on my own for once. Maybe I shouldn't have done it. . . .' She looked pensive. 'I *was* being nosy, but . . . well aren't *you* ever curious about something? I just wanted to *know* . . .'

'Know what?' demanded Andy, still cautious.

'I told you – *where* you went. If you two could see yourselves, ambling along like a couple of dreams . . . anyway, Mr Felix has nothing to do with it. When we were talking just now he was asking me if the Eccles boys had been rough again. He's going to put a stop to it. . . .'

'Eccles boys?'

'Those louts from the junk yard. . . .'

'You'd better not tell *them* where this place is!'

'Stupid!' retorted Molly, drawling. 'I wouldn't give them the time of day.'

'What shall we do with her?' Andy looked at Phil. Phil was frowning, trying to remember where he had heard the names Eccles before. Grandad had once spoken the name. Or had it been Mrs Partridge?

He asked Molly, 'Did you say the junk yard? Does somebody called Eccles own it?'

'Yes. A horrible big man with a soppy laugh, and he has a son called Lenny. Mr Felix says . . .'

Phil was wondering something else, now. 'Did you say he wrote books? What are they about?'

'I don't know . . . trains, or something. He used to work for the railway. I think he's digging about looking for history things – that's probably why you think he's been spying on you, or on whatever you're up to.' She gave them a suspicious look. 'Hey, it isn't anything dishonest, is it?'

'Not the way you think,' grinned Andy. He had got the

drift of Phil's question, now. The boys exchanged looks.
'Where exactly does this Mr Felix hang out?'

'Why do you want to know?'

'Because if you don't tell us, I'll twist your arm again!'

'You try it, that's all! Well, I'm not telling you the back
way, because that's *my* secret hide. Even the Eccles boys
don't know about that, yet. But Mr Felix lives in Arum
Street – the last house on the right.'

'Thanks,' said Andy. 'Now you'd better buzz off, and
mind nobody sees you leave. You've already blown this
place with your snooping about.'

'I've said I'm sorry, haven't I?'

'Not exactly, you haven't.'

'Well – sorry. Does that satisfy you?'

Andy grinned. He liked girls who stood up to him, and
he didn't think she would talk.

Standing enviously by, tongue-tied as he always was with
girls about, Phil sighed with relief.

Perhaps, at last, they were getting somewhere. And, as
he told Andy afterwards, he was pretty sure who the real
spies were. From now on they would have to watch out for
Mr Eccles and his son, Lenny.

11 An enthusiast intervenes

Mr Felix and Trevithick did not often have visitors, and Andy Smith's rap on the knocker woke them both out of their Sunday afternoon nap like a burst of machine-gun fire. It took some time for the railway enthusiast to find his slippers and straighten the cushions, then shuffle to the door.

He peered through his thick glasses at the short figures on the step, but his eyesight was sufficiently good to recognize them as the boys whom he had encountered in the churchyard, with such startling effect.

Andy grinned, looking more confident than he felt. 'Mr Felix? My name's Andy Smith and this is my friend, Phil Benson.'

The eyes looked big behind the spectacles. 'Did you say *Benson*?' The enthusiast was wide awake, now. He also noticed that Phil was hugging some slightly angular object beneath his windcheater. 'Good gracious! You don't mean . . . the tomb. . . .'

Andy nodded. 'That's Phil's family – sometimes I call him the last of the Bensons.'

'Do you, by heavens? Then, I think you had better come in.'

In Mr Felix's cosy sitting-room, Trevithick was summarily banished from his favourite spot on the settee. He gave the boys a one-eyed, resentful glare as they sat down, rather stiffly, on the edge.

'Would you like a biscuit?' enquired the enthusiast, rattling a tin. 'Chocolate.'

'Thanks. . . .' Andy was to do most of the talking. He got himself off to a brave start. 'Sir, is it right you're an author? I mean, you're interested in trains, and you write books about them?'

Mr Felix closed the tin but kept it handy. He twinkled, 'Your middle statement is correct. The answer to your first and last questions is that given, I was once told, by the eccentric gentleman who was asked whether he could play the fiddle. His reply was that he didn't know, because he hadn't tried. Well, I'm *trying* to write a book. . . .'

Andy leaned forward. 'A book about railway history?'

'Who told you about me?'

'That girl, Molly something.'

'Ah, Madame Beethoven!' The boys looked blank. 'That's just a little joke. . . . Yes, the book is to be a kind of railway history. That is, if it ever gets past the wondering to the writing. Why do you ask?'

Andy glanced at Phil, swallowed the last of his biscuits, and said, 'Well, you see, there are these old books and things . . . what we call Documents X.'

'And some queer photographs,' added Phil.

Andy nodded. 'The trouble is, we can't read them. We've been trying to for ages. The writing's bad, and there are lots of complicated drawings. Mr Felix, have you ever heard of an engine called the *Stormrider*?'

The eyes behind the thick lenses grew bigger still. The enthusiast didn't answer directly. 'If you can't understand them, won't any of your grown-up relatives help?'

Andy let Phil reply. 'We don't want them to . . . you see, it's rather a long story.'

'You want to tell me about it?' asked Mr Felix, patiently.

Phil hesitated only a moment before plunging into a full account of everything that had happened: Grandad and his secret, the family legend, the eventual discovery of the documents and their removal to a new hiding place after the arrival of Uncle Ern. He went on to mention Grandad's dying wish that only Phil, and Andy, should take charge of the contents of the trunk. While Uncle Ern was searching the house for 'Grandad's nest-egg', the boys had struggled to make sense of Ebenezer's strange bequest. They were sure that the diaries, if they could be read, would lead to a miser's hoard . . .

But Phil blushed as he used the melodramatic phrase. 'It isn't only that, though. I want to know what happened, all that time ago, and why Ebenezer went crazy, and did the things he did.'

'I see.' The enthusiast, who had listened intently to every word, did not ask where the documents were concealed, and this was the only thing the boys did not tell.

Andy said, 'We think Phil's uncle has got spies out, and they're watching us, trying to find out where the things are. We've guessed that the main spy is that junk man, old Eccles as the other kids call him. And his son, Lenny. . . .'

Mr Felix scowled, no longer benign. 'I've got a bone to pick with *them*, but that's over another matter.' The quizzical look returned. 'So you thought, because Molly told you of my interest in railways, that I might be able to help?'

Andy grinned. 'Yes . . . and we saw you looking jolly closely at the Benson tombstone!'

The old man chuckled. 'And you think it's high time I told *my* story. Well, that won't take long.' He mentioned his chance discovery of a letter referring to Ebenezer, the forgotten pioneer. 'I wanted to write a book about the old Greenwich line. When I found myself close to his house and his grave, well that was quite a turn-up for the book! Yes, after reading that letter in the museum I started digging around. Any day now, young Benson, I might have turned up on the doorstep and run straight into your Uncle! There doesn't seem to be, in any other quarter, much information about Ebenezer. At least, there wasn't . . .'

Phil began drawing the something out of his jacket. Mr

Felix eyed him shrewdly. 'Of course, if you really have some documents of historical interest they ought to be handed over to the proper authorities. . . .'

Phil's hand slid back. Authorities were killers of secrets and mysteries.

The white eyebrows went up. 'On the other hand, what better "authority" than the Last of the Bensons?'

Phil smiled. 'It's one of Ebenezer's diaries.'

Mr Felix took the slim book as though it were one of the Dead Sea scrolls and might immediately disintegrate. '*One*, you said. There are others?'

'Two more, and a lot of old textbooks, a cash book, some plans and drawings, and some old photos.'

The enthusiast whistled. Then he leafed, silent and fascinated for a few moments, through the diary. 'The photographs . . . do you happen to know if the images are back to front?'

'Yes!' said Phil. 'How did you guess?'

'From their apparent age I thought they might be daguerreotypes. Named after the Frenchman who first invented the process. Primitive, but the details are good?'

'Very – much better than a lot of modern ones.'

'Hm! I don't know if Ebenezer left a fortune behind, lad. But it sounds as if you're sitting on some of the most exciting discoveries of the decade. Worth a lot of money, too. . . .'

'I don't care much about that,' said Phil, quickly.

'Truth for truth's sake, eh?'

Andy said, 'Do you reckon you can read that stuff, Mr Felix?'

'A bit like Chinese, isn't it?' grumbled the enthusiast. 'You'll have to give me time.'

'What about the rest?'

'Let them lie where they are for the present, if they're safe.'

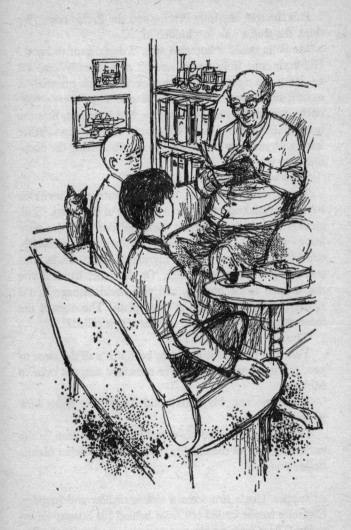

Phil thought of Molly Perkins and the Eccles boys. 'We think the stuff's safe. It's hidden in . . .'

Mr Felix raised a horrified arm. 'I don't want to know.' His brain was fully awake now. 'I'm not really sure I'd be doing the right thing, tampering with such material. A most delicate matter – probably illegal. Then there's your uncle, young Benson. Whether we like it or not, he's the head of the family, now. Of course, if your grandfather left a will, properly witnessed, specifically leaving the documents to you . . .'

'They've never found a will.'

'I was rather afraid of that.' He watched Trevithick having a wash and brush-up in a corner of the room. 'Still, giraffes that don't stick their necks out don't get the juicy leaves, do they? Give me a day or two with this gibberish, and I'll have matters clear in my mind.' Then, finally, impatience got the better of him. 'On the other hand, if you *did* happen to be passing, and you could manage it, I'd rather like to take a peep at those plans. The ones of the locomotive you mentioned . . . what was it called?'

'The *Stormrider*?' said Phil.

'Yes. And perhaps it would be best, if it's all the same to you, not to mention that you've consulted me, not even to Molly. . . .'

'Of course not, Mr Felix,' said Andy. 'We know how to keep secrets.'

The enthusiast rolled his eyes. 'That, young man, is the understatement of the century! What about another biscuit before you go?'

At supper, Uncle Ern seemed almost mellow and friendly. Cigarette smoke curled out from behind his Sunday newspaper. There were no stares, no questions, despite the fact that Phil had been out of the house for several hours.

Phil felt uneasy. Had his uncle made some new discovery? Had he seen the Eccles man that day, for instance, and learned where the Cave was? Perhaps, after all, that girl Molly Perkins had 'grassed' on them. Or the Eccles boys may have spotted her on her way back the day before and bullied the truth out of her.

Whatever Uncle Ern had discovered, if anything, he had evidently not discussed it with Aunt Luce. Phil and she had a short conversation in the kitchenette as she washed the cups.

Aunt Luce was still inclined to get Phil slightly out of focus age-wise. She chatted on about a new home perm she was going to try out, as though expecting Phil to be interested in all the pros and cons.

The she suddenly went to the other extreme, gave him a peck on the forehead and said, 'Off to bed you go, young man. Don't forget to clean your teeth. Sweet dreams!'

Phil met the old Bensons in his sleep more and more often. No two dreams ever followed exactly the same course. Even the beginnings varied.

Sometimes it was like the first dream, the making of that eerie rendezvous with Elizabeth at the viaduct arch. The circular train would rattle overhead, shedding dappled light through hard bricks; then would come again the muffled crawl through something like a wooden tunnel, with the dream-child breathing unseen in front.

There were dreams in which he arrived at a later point in the sequence; or there would be no sequence, only fragments, like the episodes from a film cut up and presented in the wrong order. There were occasions (if they could rightly be called occasions) when Phil found himself pitched straight into the cluttered scullery, or into the front parlour. Sometimes it was day time and sometimes night, with a lamp casting long, lean shadows.

Time and again Phil opened his eyes upon a new day with his head seething with the events of the dreams. Sometimes, although he was quite certain he had dreamed, what had 'happened' stayed blank behind him, or left only faint impressions like scribblings in invisible ink. But often, later in the day, the dreams would slip unexpectedly into his memory, joltingly stark and clear.

Phil, trying to solve riddles beyond understanding, could only wonder whether the dreams had a *meaning*. Or were they, like other dreams, inconsequentially put together out of long-forgotten incidents, phrases and feelings which his brain-cells flung together, as suggestive but unreal as hastily erected scenery on a dream-stage – where a charade of the long-dead past was enacted?

The Benson scullery, for instance, with its heavy, unmodern paraphernalia: had mangles been invented in 1840? Were stone coppers in use then? Or were these, too, because Phil did not know the answers, mere improvisations which the dreams used to fill in gaps?

At least the old, old Bensons seemed real. Though they were always dressed in the unsuitable Sabbath costumes of the marvellously vivid photographs, they moved freely and naturally about their week-day lives. They spoke, ate, laughed . . . they came and went through doors, took off boots in the scullery, sat down to meals. Phil always seemed to be one of them, bowing his head as grace was said, awaiting his turn at table, listening to conversations which, however, were remembered only as fragmentary echoes. 'Scottie won't be back till Thursday,' or 'I told Jessup, don't buy a pig in a poke.'

And the view from the parlour windows: wasn't that, Phil asked himself, the scene in his old viaduct print wonderfully, mysteriously transferred and hung against the backcloth of his sleep? The sounds: shoutings, barkings, the whistle of the squat train drawn upon the flat, ice-blue sky . . . were they *actual* sounds heard through his bedroom window while he lay betwixt sleeping and waking?

And in the midst of all the doubts, the questions, the self-mockery, a tiny voice deep in Phil's heart would persist: yes! There *is* meaning, there *is* a reality. Wait!

Perhaps he should discuss the dreams with someone else, someone wiser, or someone whose different way of thinking might help to make things clearer. Aunt Luce? No. Mr Felix? Not yet. Andy? No, no! Andy would be intrigued, of course, but he'd be full of facile, 'scientific' explanations. He'd talk, chortling, about his own dreams; the sort in which one races across a rooftop in one's pyjamas, or wins a fabulous prize in a TV competition. Andy would demand something solid to support any hint from Phil that he believed ... well, that in some unfathomable manner, he *had* met the old Bensons.

Without at least one solid clue, Andy would snuff out that small voice deep inside Phil. It would die of ridicule.

12 Prams to the rescue

Lenny Eccles was like his father in appearance – big, powerfully built, squash-nosed – and he had large, strong hands with the nails worn down short and ragged, and red with rust from old metal.

Lenny had several of his gang with him, mostly younger boys. They were all being addressed, late one afternoon, by Mr Eccles in the ramshackle tin shed where piles of wheels, girders and junk of all kinds awaited collection by the bigger scrap dealers who had uses for such things.

'You're a dim lot of beggars, aren't you? You ought to have cottoned on to their hideout by now.'

Lenny shifted to another foot. He said, defensively, 'Them boys are dead crafty. I reckon they know we're on to them. Every time they see us around, they scarpa.'

'Then they don't get a chance to see you, right? You want to use a bit of savvy. And concentrate on the job in hand, instead of wasting your time needling that Perkins girl and those titches.'

Lenny felt the eyes of his henchmen on him and tried to worm out of the spot he was in. 'We reckon she has something to do with this lark. We saw her talking to them boys yesterday – through these.'

He glanced down at the old pair of binoculars strapped round his shoulder. Mr Eccles was not impressed. 'That don't prove a thing. Still, you want to get on to her and find out, don't you?'

'Yeah, we will.'

'But don't go making a big deal out of it. We don't want this business being squawked all round. And lay off the titches – just quiz the Perkins girl in a round-about sort of way.'

Lenny nodded, his dark brows scowling. 'Okay. All the same, it would be easier if we knew what we was looking for exactly. I mean, what's *in* this hideout?'

Mr Eccles spat a shred of tobacco out of his mouth, and grinned. 'None of your business. All we've got to remember is that there may be a quid or two coming your way if a certain party I know gets the information he wants. A quid or two each, that is,' he added, looking round the circle. 'Just find the place where the boys go. It must be one of the arches.'

'There are hundreds of them,' complained Lenny.

'Not between here and the last footbridge. If it was farther than that, those kids wouldn't bother to come this way to get there, would they? Especially if they've guessed they're being watched. They'd go round by the streets.'

A substitute for intelligence brightened Lenny's eyes. 'Yeah, that's true.'

'You could go along there and try all the doors. You might find one that ain't locked up properly. I'd do it myself, but it might look suspicious. Nobody takes much notice of a bunch of boys mucking about down there.'

Lenny wondered about the motives behind this excuse. But he contented himself with a sullen nod. Then he took his gang off to work out some sort of fresh plan.

The following day, at about the same time, Molly was making her way to the hide. There was a birthday party at the flats, and only one of her brothers, Jimmy, was with her. Jimmy was six, and it was his idea that they went to Mr Felix's. Mr Felix had hinted that, if there weren't too many of them at once, there might be some chocolate biscuits going free.

As usual, when Molly reached the point where she

turned off into the labyrinthine route to the 'jungle', she gave a sharp look round to see whether any of the Eccles boys were about. When she saw that they were, also as usual, she carried out a sly detour and headed in a different direction.

She didn't like the way the boys – there were four of them this time – increased their stride to catch her up. There were no taunts, just a casual encirclement forcing her and Jimmy to stop.

Lenny said, grinning, 'We want to do you a favour.'

'Beat it!'

'Now, don't be like that.' The voice was mincing, the eyes faintly menacing. 'You can listen, can't you?'

'If I have to.'

'You have to.' He waited for a train to hurtle past on the tracks overhead. 'We've got an offer.'

'We don't want anything from you.'

'Protection. A sort of arrangement, see? I tell my gang to lay off, and we all chum up nice and cosy. We don't even come and wreck your hideout. We know where you go, you and those snotty-nosed kids you cart about.' He knew nothing of the kind, but it was useful to pretend that he did. 'It would be a pity if they was to be upset. Now, if you had protection . . .'

Molly flushed. 'You wouldn't dare! We have permission to go there. Mr Felix lets us.'

'Who's Mr Felix?' The name was unfamiliar to Lenny. He stored it away, it could be important.

'You'll find out if you go chucking nuts and bolts about in his garden!' Too late, Molly saw the gleam in Lenny's eyes, the sidelong glance he gave his gang. 'What – what am I expected to do to be protected? Pay protection money?'

The criminal jargon was something she had heard on TV. Lenny grinned. 'No, not money. Just a bit of information. You're pally with them two boys, aren't you? Phil Benson and Andy Smith?'

Molly's heart jumped. 'Not particularly.'

'No, but I mean, you know where their hideout, or camp, or whatever they call it, is?'

Molly hesitated too long. 'What are you talking about?'

'I reckon you know.'

Desperately, Molly tried to play for time. Her inquisitiveness had penetrated to the Cave, but no farther. She had no idea why first Phil and Andy, and now the Eccles boys, attached such importance to what was no more than a mere game. Or *was* it a game? Had Molly, somehow, got herself mixed up in something more sinister?

'Let me past!'

None of them budged. A skinny, grey-faced boy was muttering, 'Why don't we just give them a good doing over and drag the truth out of them?'

Lenny ignored the suggestion. 'All right. You think it over. We'll give you till tomorrow.' A new strategem occurred to him. Phil's Uncle Ern, had he been present, would have applauded. 'What's in the place, anyway?'

'Nothing! Except . . .' Molly bit her lip.

'So you do know where it is! You must even have seen it. You're a lying little madam, aren't you?'

'I'm not. Let us go.' She was conscious of Jimmy's hand anxiously clutching her own. 'I – I'll meet you here tomorrow, at the same time. I'll come on my own.'

Lenny glanced at Jimmy. 'I get it. You mean, when you haven't got little big-ears with you? Okay. But don't try nothing cute beforehand. We're going to watch you, baby.'

The gangsterish threat, in Lenny's opinion, would add force to his warning.

'What else could I do?'

Andy nodded grudgingly. He had known from the start,

he thought, that the girl would mess things up somehow.

'I don't know what all this is about, but I'm willing to help, if you want me.'

'What about tomorrow, when you meet the Eccles lot?'

'I shan't meet them. I'll stay at home.'

'That'll be a lot of use! If you don't turn up, they'll smell a rat.'

Phil walked beside them, but not of them, along the high street. He had a sense of inadequacy. Others were getting so involved. *His* secret was becoming a gigantic snowball, rushing down a mountain, threatening an avalanche of revelation. And his own thoughts were not geared to this surface, slick exchange between Andy and the girl.

Molly had found them heading for the Cave, after the encounter with Lenny. She'd sent Jimmy on home and steered Phil and Andy through the alley and over the road bridge into town. The bustle of traffic and shops provided the best sort of hiding-place just now.

Andy asked, 'Have you got any money?'

'A bit. Why?'

'Run off and buy yourself a lolly or something. Then come back. I want to talk to Phil.'

She went without protest.

Andy said, 'The Eccles boys are bound to find the Cave, now. It's only a matter of time. We've got to get Documents X out and take them to Mr Felix.'

'He hasn't agreed to read them, yet.'

Andy grinned. 'He will. You should have seen his eyes pop when I took him the *Stormrider* plans.'

Andy had done so on his way home from school the previous day.

'We'd still better make sure.'

'Okay, what's wrong with now? We'll shake Molly off first. She may be able to help later. I've half an idea already, but we'll have to talk to Mr Felix before we do anything.'

Mr Felix waved the *Stormrider* plans exuberantly in their faces. 'This is stupendous! You boys have been sitting on a discovery that will set every railway enthusiast in the country by his ears. It's like coming across a lost fresco by Michelangelo, an unknown play by Shakespeare, a tenth symphony of Beethoven. See here. . . .'

He spread the crackling sheet on the floor and knelt beside it. He gasped and spluttered on and on, trying to explain the complex drawings – reaching up for spoons and plates and almost anything else within reach and putting them together to demonstrate things called piston thrusts and pre-heating systems and torques and pressures. Phil and Andy were soon hopelessly lost.

'Don't you see? The Stephensons had not progressed so far a decade later . . . most of the secret is in this turret. I'm convinced that the Benson system would have worked most efficiently. It would have influenced locomotive development all the way down the years. . . .'

The stubby fingers darted like wolf spiders over Ebenezer's old parchment which, by now, was becoming liberally sprayed with enthusiastic little specks of saliva. Andy interrupted, 'But Mr Felix, the diary. . . .'

'Yes, yes – the diary. Most fascinating sketches in the margins, you know. And I've actually been able to decipher some of the technical data. . . .'

'Anything about . . . anything else?' asked Phil.

Mr Felix, sitting back cross-legged on the floor, looked faintly puzzled. 'Oh, you mean Ebenezer Benson's private affairs? Give me time, my boy. I haven't so far dwelt on anything of a trivial nature. I expect most of the personal stuff *is* trivial. People who write diaries often include such a great deal that is unimportant – even Samuel Pepys was guilty of that. And Ebenezer's writing . . . heavens, it's like Outer Mongolian, written backwards and upside down. I've hardly slept since Saturday.'

'If we bring the rest,' said Phil, 'please will you read them?'

'If I live long enough,' sighed the enthusiast, sadly. 'Mum's the word, mind! We must be discreet ... but, you know, I do feel that Destiny has singled us out to restore Ebenezer Benson to his rightful place in the records. ...'

Destiny! For Phil the word had a poignant, meaningful ring – like a bell's echo. Mr Felix went on, his eyebrows meeting as he scanned the drawings. 'If only he had built it. If *only* ... What *could* have gone wrong?' He shook his head and looked back at the boys. 'Now, how do you intend to fetch the other documents to me?'

At first, Andy's plan sounded idiotic and dangerous. Even Phil, who had once carried out a similar operation almost singlehanded, thought that the risks were enormous. 'Why can't we simply do what we did before – use the chest-of-drawers and wheel it in your go-cart?'

'Because everything's different, now. We'd either have to bring it along the path at this end, and that would mean passing Eccles's yard. Or, if we tried to push it the long way round, we'd have to heave it up those bridges and we'd be spotted. Molly says that Lenny carries binoculars.'

'In that case they'll see Molly, and after what happened the other night they'll never let her through.'

'I've thought of that, naturally. Molly meets us at the Cave tomorrow afternoon. Unless Lenny's glasses can see round corners, he won't spot us there from the junk yard. Molly brings this pram, see? It has a real baby in it! She reckons she can fix it with the kid's mum. It's a big pram, with one of those collapsible steps in the bottom for when the kid's old enough to sit up and stick his feet in. We could stow most of the stuff under the mattress.'

'What about the rest?'

'Ah, that's the subtle part,' said Andy, proudly. 'A couple

of the little kids will bring their dolls' prams. They'll hold
the diaries and the photograph cases . . . what's the matter
now?'

Phil's face had turned pale. 'It's the thought of Ebenezer's
papers, being carted along in a lot of prams – by kids!
Suppose they meet the Eccles lot?'

'We hope they don't,' said Andy, airily. 'With a bit of
luck it may be raining. That'll keep 'em indoors.'

'But if it rains. . . .'

'The baby will get wet, not the papers! And if Lenny
Eccles does meet them, he won't suspect anything. Molly's
brother, the oldest one, Tommy, will be with them. If
Lenny tries to stop Molly, Tommy will push the pram on
and take the little kids with him, straight to Mr Felix's
garden. They won't bother with a lot of kids and a baby.
They'll just want to talk to Molly. Molly will stall them
as long as she can, and by that time, we'll be home and
dry.' Andy grinned. 'Well, how's that?'

'And we're going to push off, after we've locked the
Cave, and go to Mr Felix's the front way?'

'Right! The Eccles lot won't connect us with the procession. If they're watching anything, all they'll see is the
kids making for their hide as usual. What can go wrong?'

Practically everything, decided Phil, gloomily. But he
could think of no better plan of his own. And he had to
admit that making several furtive journeys with the precious
documents and books tucked under their jackets was more
likely to meet with disaster.

Next day, it was almost as if Andy had appeased some
ancient household god of his own, for the rain fell. Phil had
brought some polythene bags in which to wrap the documents. They got them stacked into the prams. Molly held
the baby, still asking no questions about what the mysterious packages contained.

The procession set off along the muddy viaduct path.

The Viaduct

The baby cooed happily beneath his waterproof hood. Phil watched them anxiously for a moment, then let Andy pull him away towards the steps.

The procession had steps to climb, too, but Molly was practically as strong as any boy, and she and her two younger brothers were able to deal with the prams one by one. Back on the flat, they carefully avoided the broken

bottles and squelched on. As they drew nearer the Eccles's yard, Molly kept her eyes down – willing herself not to look up at the tottery tin wall of the shed.

Through a hole in the corrugated iron, Lenny Eccles watched. He saw the caravan of children and prams heading for the jungle, as though hurrying in from the rain.

He grinned, enjoying the discomfort of others. Then, slowly, he swung the glasses back to the vacant viaduct path.

13 A thin, black penny

The latest dream was like a play seen some time ago, then half forgotten. The star rôle had been played by Timothy Benson. Timothy had cried. Phil could not remember a hoop, but the collie had been around, the dog whose barks were so often transmuted into the restless night growls of some mongrel in a yard past Phil's window.

Awakening with a sense of the dream's importance in his mind, Phil strove to recall why Timothy had cried. He was half dressed before he remembered. Of course! Timothy had wept because he had lost a penny – the penny Phil had given him to buy sweets.

There was no one to see the stark, comprehending look that froze Phil's face: nor the frantic way he searched the table top beside his bed, the pockets of his clothes, then, as a last resort (yet, now he had thought of it, wasn't this the obvious place?) the jacket pocket of his pyjamas.

He did not find what he was looking for.

It was the Sunday after the delivery of Documents X to Arum Street, a couple of hours after Phil's awakening, and Aunt Luce and Uncle Ern had driven off to shop for bargains at a street market. Aware of Uncle Ern's faint disapproval, Phil had declined to accompany them. When their exhaust died away round the corner, he went, very slowly, downstairs. He had no clear idea of what he wished to do: it was simply as if the old house, vacant around him, was urging him on.

He began with the parlour, now glittering and showy with Uncle Ern's bargain furniture and fittings. Defiantly, the tall, narrow window looked out on the wet pavements, the forbidding faces of the houses opposite and then, not far beyond, the stretch of grey viaduct. There was little here to hold Phil's interest. He turned along the short passage beside the staircase, down a single step and into the kitchen. Here, too, were the fruits of Uncle Ern's spending; his tasteless, obvious efforts to keep Aunt Luce contented now that he had wrenched her away from the little bungalow in Luton. A sickly green sink unit, already scratched on delivery, clung beneath the taps by the window. A wall cabinet with sliding glass panels enclosed the crockery; there was a cream electric cooker and a still unpainted shelf supporting pots and pans. . . .

And, on the other side, the stairs side, there stood a white enamelled, unmatching washing machine and spin drier, no doubt purchased separately, on the cheap, from a different dealer.

Phil peered behind it. The stumps of old pipes stuck out of the wall like amputated limbs. Faintly he remembered that a copper had once stood here. He remembered his mother stooping down, reaching awkwardly, to put a match to the gas, the sometimes alarming *pop!* that had followed. Phil himself now reached behind the washing machine and gave a sharp rap on the wall.

It was hollow! He felt confused. Was he thinking of the dream, the crawl with Elizabeth along a wooden tunnel, and their arrival at this very point? Had an even more primitive copper, all steam and stone, once stood here? And the hollow wall . . . or, rather, the cavity behind it . . . how had he known, just now, about its existence?

It was the stair-well, of course. The stairs started back there in the passage, but over this corner of the kitchen, which had once been a scullery, the cavity rose high, as high as the landing upstairs. Was it still possible to get into it?

Phil went back into the passage. He saw the wooden

door, newly painted and of triangular shape, following the rise of the staircase. And he remembered the first day, when he had been very young, that he had explored the cupboard under the stairs. He'd found the triangular door half open, had crawled inside, picking his way excitedly through the boxes and brushes and rolled-up lengths of carpet and all kinds of junk. At the far end, in almost pitch darkness, he had found himself in a lofty, uncluttered space. Cobwebs had brushed against his face and he'd suddenly grown terribly frightened. Frantically he'd banged the wooden wall beside him. There had come answering raps, a muffled voice.

Phil had crawled back hastily, tears of alarm smarting in his eyes. He had got himself entangled with the junk, had somehow gone right past the door and into the narrow, tight space beneath the lower stairs. There, struggling against stark terrors, he had been rescued by his mother. 'What a state you're in, silly boy! The glory hole's no place for you.'

The glory hole! Phil smiled as he remembered his mother's name for the cupboard.

He went upstairs for his torch, returned, opened the cupboard door and crawled inside. It was still a depository of junk and domestic equipment. Aunt Luce's new vacuum cleaner, still in its cardboard carton, rolls of carpeting, brushes and brooms. But a swish of the torch beam showed that the place had been thoroughly cleaned. Not a single cobweb wafted on the zig-zag understairs. Half-way along was Grandad's – Ebenezer's – tin trunk with its lid broken and twisted, the old clothing no longer inside. Phil shone his torch on it for a moment, as though in salute, then raised the beam and saw the timbers beneath the landing. Nothing stood here.

He came back towards the narrower part, until, with the gas and electric meters on his right, he had to stoop low and crawl. And there, beside some packets of detergent and bottles, his knees creaked on loose boards.

Phil saw that the nails were missing, yet there were still sets of small holes, edged with rust. The boards had been prised up at some time, then replaced loosely on their supporting beams. It was easy to get his fingers under the edge of one, raise it, then remove the others. He thrust the short planks into a hasty pile and shone his torch into the emptiness below.

The stench came up, dry, sour and stale. Four feet down, dusty, brick-bestrewn soil lay with an undisturbed look, its particles too dry for the marks of definite prints. Phil got his feet through, gripped the torch in his teeth and lowered himself on his elbows. Kneeling in the sand-like dust, he flicked the torch beam to and fro. On all sides were short, thick walls, with pipes and wires following tortuous routes beneath the floors. There were breaks in the foundation walls on which the old house stood, allowing access from one part of the foundations to another. Some way to Phil's left, below the front room, daylight twinkled through the holes of a ventilation grille. The shadow of a passing vehicle blinked across it.

Here and there were little bits of rubbish and unimportant, mildly intriguing relics. He found a small piece of paper, part of an invoice, or similar document, headed with a name: F. Janders & Son. The writing on it was in pencil and had to do with the replacement of some water pipes. There was a multiplication sum: 23 times 9 = 197. Wrong answer! It was scribbled in pencil. The date of the sheet was 5 August 1929.

Not far away was a cigarette packet of a brand unfamiliar to Phil, who had once collected packets. Had it been discarded, all that time ago, by the workman who couldn't do sums?

The next discovery was more ominous: a foil tobacco

wrapping, still with brown shreds clinging to it, the kind Uncle Ern smoked. Of course! Uncle Ern had removed those boards. *He* had been down here during his search of the house. Although Phil had half guessed this, he felt slightly deflated, like an astronaut landing on the moon and finding a rival flag already planted in the dust. And Grandad, and other Bensons before him, had they been here on the hunt for Ebenezer's hoard? Was it down here that the lodger, the Irishman, O'Reilly, had been asked to probe and look out for something of value?

There were no answers to these questions now. Phil turned back for the hole in the floor, his fingers scrabbling in the dust ... and it was then that he found the penny. It was black with age, thin, the surfaces pitted. Thinking of it as a small curiosity, dropped by the workman, perhaps, Phil was about to slip it into his pocket. Then, as he glanced closer at it in the light from his torch, he gave a little cry of amazement, of disbelief. The head ... the date, barely discernible, when his hot hand turned the coin over. . . .

'Are you saying that, when you fall asleep, you get into a sort of *time machine*?'

Phil sighed. He had been saying nothing of the kind. At last he had told Andy about the dreams, saving the penny tight in his hand till the end. Andy had listened patiently, lounging back in the tattered old car seat which was the Cave's most recent acquisition. Once or twice he had smiled, then straightened his face when he saw how deadly serious Phil was.

The handing over of the penny had been intended as a climax, a clincher; but Andy's face was disappointingly unimpressed. 'No,' said Phil. 'Not a time machine, exactly. A sort of – of . . .'

There he was stuck. Andy was, apparently, quite prepared to discuss the possible existence of some vague gadget, all wires and terminals and transistors, that somehow clipped itself to the frame of Phil's bed at nightfall. But *dreaming* into the past was highly unmechanized and therefore unacceptable.

Andy looked again at the thin coin, not offering to return it. 'Let's get this straight . . . these dreams of yours, they're in instalments, like a T V series?'

Phil did not smile. 'In a way. But things don't always happen in the right order. I mean, sometimes I dream bits that must have happened *before* the bits I dreamed earlier. D'you get it?'

Andy tried to get it. 'And the Bensons talk to you?'

'Yes. They used to be all fuzzy, but that's improving. It's funny, but they seem to accept me, as if I was one of them.'

'They would.'

'How d'you mean?'

'Well, they're your dreams, aren't they? Everybody in them comes out of your head.'

'But that's just the point. *Do* they? They always seem . . . well, seem to be living their lives, and doing their everyday ordinary things as though I wasn't around.' A particular incident came to Phil's mind, and he went on, broodingly: 'I remember once, Ebenezer arguing with old Steve. I don't know what it was about, but I can see them now . . . Ebenezer was terribly angry. He was standing near the window and the sun shone on his face and his shadow looked all hunched. He kept banging on the table with his fist, and some pots of plants shook on the shelf behind him. . . .'

'Those windows . . . have you ever tried to go outside?'

'No . . . it's only a sort of picture world. I told you . . .'

'But *they* go outside.'

'The Bensons? Yes. At least they *seem* to.'

'Then why can't you?'

'I never think of it in the dreams. Sometimes I promise myself I'll do things. I concentrate hard before falling asleep and I say, "Tonight, I'll open the scullery door and see what's outside" – things like that. But in the dreams, I don't remember.'

Andy risked a grin. 'Why don't you write yourself a list of instructions, and pin them to your pyjamas?'

Phil thought about it, solemnly, not realizing that Andy was teasing him. 'I don't think I *am* wearing pyjamas, in the dreams. That would be rather daft, wouldn't it? I mean, the Bensons would think it odd. . . .'

'What are you wearing, then?'

'I've never noticed. . . .' Phil stared at the candle, the thoughts whirling. 'The same as boys *did* wear in those days, I suppose. Clothes like Jamie's. . . .'

'Posh ones, like in the photos?'

'I don't know. It's funny – did I tell you? I've never actually seen Jamie in the dreams. . . .'

But Andy was flipping the coin. 'Now tell me about this penny. You found it under the floorboards at home.'

'Yes . . . and it was only last night that I dreamed the bit about Timothy.'

'You gave him a penny?'

'That's it. He was howling about something, and we couldn't stop him. You know how it is with kids . . . I gave him a penny to buy sweets.'

'What did he do?'

'Stopped howling. Then he dropped the penny and it rolled off somewhere. That made him cry again. I got down and tried to look for it . . . but everything came over muzzy then, and I woke up.'

'And you reckon it's *your* penny you've found?'

'Well, you see, I had a new penny. I got it from a shop with some change and it was all shiny, so I tried not to spend it. You know how you do. Well, the last I can remember I had it either on my bedside table or . . .'

'In your pyjama pocket?'

'Yes!'

'But you said you didn't wear pyjamas in your dreams.'

'I know. I'm not trying to explain it. I'm only saying . . .'

'Didn't your Timothy notice anything queer about the coin when you gave it to him?'

'No. I said, he dropped it. What are you grinning at now?'

'You cheated him! Pennies were a lot bigger than this in eighteen-forty odd.' He saw Phil glare at this untimely display of general knowledge and hurried on, 'Anyway, if the penny just rolled off down a crack in the floor and has lain there ever since, why is it thin and corroded with age? You said you found that piece of paper, dated nineteen-twenty-nine, and could still read a pencilled sum. It takes moisture, and thousands of people's rubbing fingers, to wear a coin thin.'

Phil put his chin in his hands. 'I know. But our house hasn't always been exactly as it is now. There *may* have been a time when the penny lay for years in the wet. Or it may have been found, and handled, then lost again . . . and you still haven't explained why a coin in such a state has Queen Elizabeth the Second's head on it, and this year's date!'

Andy turned the penny over as if expecting to find the answer engraved there along with the other perplexing data. 'It doesn't *have* to be age. It could be a different penny, not yours. And somebody dropped it in some acid, or in the fire. I bet if we took it to a chemist he could tell us whether it was really old or not. They've got ways, now, of telling the dates of fossils. It's called the carbon test, and . . .'

132

'Oh, give it to me!'

Phil snatched the coin back, squeezed it in his fist and returned it to his pocket.

Andy's grin was almost a leer. 'You're scared of the truth!'

Phil gripped his fists, feeling the thin edge of the penny bite into his flesh. 'What do *you* know about the truth?' he retorted.

And their friendship nearly died.

On their next visit to Arum Street, Phil saw the photograph cases spread out on the sideboard next to some of the technical books. Trevithick sat beside them, flicking his tail, as though on guard. His single watery eye looked baleful when Phil nudged him away.

Mr Felix peered over Phil's shoulder. 'Definitely daguerreotypes, just as I surmised. Most remarkable. I wonder how Ebenezer got hold of the equipment? The little chap with the hoop, and the dog, must have got in by mistake. The process required a very long time exposure by modern standards, and that accounts for the hazy effect. They wouldn't have been able to pin that young man down long enough to have his portrait done properly.'

After this it was difficult to pin Mr Felix to anything, either. He looked weary and dishevelled, the shock of white hair brushed out in all directions, but his eyes were bright with a knowledge that he seemed reluctant to share.

'Have – have you found out much?' asked Andy.

'Hum ... yes and no.' After this unsatisfactory answer the enthusiast slumped into his chair and fiddled for a while with his pipe. Several matches flared, and were consumed, before he said, 'Getting impatient, are you? I suppose you're afraid of what your uncle may find out soon. Madame Beethoven tells me that the Eccles gang are becoming even nastier than usual. So far I've managed to chase them away from the top of my garden, but they know she comes there.'

'They're stupid,' declared Andy, contemptuously. 'They haven't even found the Cave, yet.'

'The *what*?'

Phil said, 'It's what we call the arch where we hid the papers – under the viaduct.'

'Oh! Well, I guessed it must be some such place. Not that it matters any longer so far as the documents are concerned.'

Andy persisted. 'But have you *read* them, Mr Felix?'

The enthusiast nodded ruefully at the table on which, beside an old leather dispatch case in which he stored the more fragile of Ebenezer's papers, were several plates containing the remains of meals and at least four unwashed cups and saucers. 'My boy, I've been eating and sleeping on the job for three days and nights. As for the diaries, I'm half way through the year eighteen-forty-three. Fascinating ... quite fascinating. I'm beginning to wonder...'

The pause was so long that the boys thought that Mr Felix had dropped off to sleep. Then he suddenly opened his eyes, blinked tantalizingly at Phil, and went on, 'I'm beginning to wonder whether, if the Last of the Bensons would agree, we ought to call in some expert advice. Certain discreet friends of mine. . . .'

'To help read the diaries?' frowned Phil.

'Oh, no – I'm coping with that. It's what the diaries *say*.'

'But – but *what* do they say?'

Mr Felix closed his eyes again. 'I'd rather wait a bit before telling you that. You might, however, prepare yourselves for a little surprise!'

The reopened eyes were large but unrevealing.

14 'I am Jamie'

That night, as Phil lay trying to get off to sleep, Mr Felix's words kept echoing again and again in his mind: 'It's what the diaries say ... prepare yourselves for a little surprise.' Then the enthusiast's friendly, mild face, with the gentle eyes glowing big behind the spectacles, became as wise and secretive as an owl's.

The train on the viaduct, too, hooted like an owl, and a thought, elusive but compelling, accompanied Phil's drift into slumber. ...

The dream was quite different from any of the others: far more real, far more like a wakeful experience. There was no rendezvous with Elizabeth, no dusty crawl through a wooden tunnel and emergence from behind a stone copper. Neither was there the madly whirling circular train: no throbbing in his ears, or fuzziness of senses. ...

It was a spring day and the sun was warm on his face, for he was out of doors. At last he had gained access to the mysterious picture-frame world of the newly built viaduct, but the picture had burst and blossomed into life. A real breeze moved the trees, touching his hair and sending fallen petals scurrying along the paved way at his feet. A bird sang. Then, coming slowly along the railway above, a train hooted upon a strange yet familiar note.

Phil walked along until he was suddenly in the midst of a great activity. He had an impression of an immense, stone ramp rising beyond his feet to high parapets. Workmen in thick boots, rough spoken, grimy faced, toiled at stout trucks laden with objects of metal. There was much clanging of iron. One group sat on barrels, sipping from tin mugs and biting into slabs of bread, and it was one of these fellows who grinned and waved at Phil, his recognition half jocular, half deferential.

There was the subtlest shift in the dream.... Phil was inside some yawning cavern of a place. There were spiral steps leading down, down ... and at the bottom a heavy wood door yielded to his push. Beyond the door was darkness out of which phantom shapes formed themselves: wheels, boilers, funnels writhing in smoke shrouds. Then there was light, the sudden, unsteady light of flares: and within that broad, windowless place smelling of oil and fire, the white faces of men turned in his direction like moons amidst constellations of flying sparks.

Ebenezer Benson – undoubtedly he, though he was no longer dressed in the Sabbath clothes of the photograph – came anxiously towards Phil. His grip on the boy's shoulders was firm but not unkind; he was merely turning Phil away. 'Tha hast no business here, lad. Wait for me at th' top and say nowt o' what tha'st seen.'

Phil did as he was bidden, reclimbed the dark stairway and walked alone into the blinding sunlight. He walked on along the path, away from the clangour and smell of engines. Amidst the open arches close to the rustling elms was peace: Phil breathed the sweet air from the river and was aware of pain – always pain – clutching deep within his chest....

Inside one of the open arches he found a short length of iron spike, something thrown there, discarded. He picked it up. At first idly, then with deepening concentration while time crept by, he began to carve in the clean brickwork. He carved and carved until a little pile of reddish-brown dust formed at his feet ... J.B. 1843.

He had just finished when Ebenezer Benson spoke close beside him: 'Come away, then, *Jamie* lad. I'll take thee home....'

There was an instant between sleeping and waking when Phil thought, 'I am Jamie Benson. I have been brought home and now I am in bed, dying. I can hear angels singing.'

Then he sat up, wide awake. The solemn words his memory had dredged from some sad, old story book faded away. He was *Phil* Benson – not Jamie. The room was grey and early and it was the birds that were singing.

The dawn chorus: chirrupings and pipings and whistlings hung about the house like curtains of sound. It was as though a canopy of feathered things, wing-tip to wing-tip, domed the morning sky. Yet when Phil tiptoed to the window he saw only damp, grey rooftops hazy with mist.

He sat on the edge of his bed for a while. He took the thin, black penny from beneath his pillow and turned it over and over in his hand. His thoughts plunged so deep that they almost became new dreams. His eyes fell on the print of the old viaduct and for a moment he was back there amidst the arches.... When he had left the forbidden staircase, how far had he walked? How far – how *far?*

He dressed quickly, pulling on old clothes, lacing plimsolls on his feet. He left the house through the carefully unbolted back door, climbed the brick wall at the foot of the garden and raced to the corner. At the telephone kiosk he paused, waiting for a solitary car to pass in the misty street. Then he crossed, his footsteps slower.

In a shop doorway he paused again, and this time it was the traffic of his own thoughts that held him back. Should he call for Andy? Could what he wanted to do be done alone?

He thought through his last dream again. Then he thought of the viaduct, and Ebenezer, and Jamie, and suddenly he had a mental picture of the angel over the Bensons' ivy-clad grave. The angel that smiled ... Andy would smile, too, if Phil dared to tell him. . . . But he need not tell of the dream. It could masquerade as an idea of his own, a new hunch. Andy would understand about hunches.

A figure hurried along the opposite pavement, carelessly dressed, slippered, face set in purpose. It opened the door of the telephone kiosk and went inside.

Phil's heart missed a beat. It was Uncle Ern! Uncle Ern had, after all, seen Phil leave the house. He had slipped out after him, not in pursuit, but in order to make a telephone call. To whom?

The junk man, Eccles, of course! Who else? Phil's skin tingled. Uncle Ern believed in hunches, too. Phil could almost fancy how it had happened. Uncle Ern waking, overhearing some stealthy movement of Phil's. Waiting, listening, stifling his morning cough, then catching a glimpse of him as he'd scrambled over the wall. He would guess that Phil was heading for his secret place in the viaduct arches. Now the junk man was being warned to watch for Phil's arrival at the Wasteland and have him followed. It was typical of Uncle Ern's devious patience, and hope, and love of setting traps. . . .

Phil slid out from the doorway, hurried round the corner and made for Andy Smith's.

'But why on earth did you come out so early? Couldn't you sleep?'

Andy had spent most of the time so far complaining about his missed breakfast. But he'd dragged on his clothes, then fallen loyally, if a trifle sullenly, into step with Phil along the brightening pavement. 'Anyway, what's the flap? The only valuable thing in the Cave now is my best car seat! Mr Felix has the papers. Why not let your uncle chuck his money away on phone calls if that'll make him happy, and go back to bed?'

'*Something's* hidden there,' said Phil.

Andy's look was suspicious. 'Have you been dreaming again?'

'It – it's a sort of hunch.'

'About Ebenezer's hoard?'

'No . . . not exactly.'

'Well, you've got me beat. So now we're going to Mr Felix's?'

'No – to the Cave.'

'You're joking, of course! Don't you realise that by this time the whole Wasteland'll be crawling with Lenny Eccles and his mob?'

'Scared?'

'Of course not!' Andy grinned. 'Anyway, aren't you? There's no sense in sticking our necks into a trap for nothing.'

'But it isn't for nothing. I think . . .' The rest of the sentence never arrived. Phil came indecisively to a standstill. 'You'll think I'm crackers if I tell you.'

'I think you're crackers anyway!' Andy had never intended the retort to bite so deep. It had slipped off his tongue, bitterly regretted but too late to retrieve.

Phil swung on his heels and ran. Before Andy had even collected his wits to follow, the lean, plimsolled figure was far away in the direction of the viaduct. Dispirited and hating himself, Andy trotted after him. By the time he had reached the white posts by the row of shops, Phil seemed to have melted among the litter of junk heaps.

'Hello!'

Molly Perkins approached. She was pushing an old bicycle. Hung on her shoulder was a canvas bag filled with newspapers. Her expression was diffident, as though she wished she hadn't run into Andy like this.

Andy asked, 'Have you seen Phil?'

'No. Why – what's happened?'

'Nothing, yet – I hope! But the Eccles gang may be waiting for him down there. He's in a daze about something, and if they track him down to the Cave and then find out there's nothing there . . .'

Molly looked at the ground. 'They know about the Cave, they found it last night.'

'They *what*?'

Molly countered Andy's stare. 'I didn't grass, if that's what you're thinking. My brother Jimmy said it was one of the other kids; one of the girls who helped with the dolls prams. Lenny Eccles must have found out about what we did, and bullied the truth out of her!'

'C-rumbs!' gasped Andy. 'Then . . . they'll be waiting for him – at the Cave.'

That same night, Mr Felix had not slept a wink. Kettle gently bubbling on his gas stove, he had topped up and stirred the tea in its pot until it became as thick as soup. When he had something big on his mind, Mr Felix did not think of his bed. The extra hours of consciousness were useful to an enthusiast; they made life seem to last a little longer.

By the early hours of the morning he had picked his way, phrase by impossible phrase, through most of Ebenezer Benson's diary for 1844. Certain technical matters of considerable interest held him up for a time while he waggled his eyebrows at the margins cluttered with sketches.

'Amazing!' he said, and the word was like something small dropped into the night's silence. Trevithick opened his eye reproachfully, then purred back to sleep.

Mr Felix did not hear the rain. The dawn chorus left him unimpressed. At 6 a.m. precisely, his fist thumped hard on the table, and Trevithick almost slid off his cushion. 'Eureka!' cried the enthusiast. 'That's *it*!'

15 Stormrider story

The overnight rain had been a mere sprinkling. Down here on the viaduct path the mud was caking with the season's drying out. There were already cracks in it, branching out from wider splits like the patterns on leaves.

Phil slowed his pace before reaching the first footbridge. He was already regretting his petulant, thick-witted reaction to Andy's taunt. He glanced behind him, hoping to see Andy's ginger head bobbing up and down in pursuit. Andy was not there, and Phil wondered whether to go back, find him, and try to explain.

But explain what? That he had *guessed*, and the guess had turned into a dream, and the dream was drawing him irresistibly to the viaduct, where Ebenezer's true secret lay waiting? Yet the intense, haunted mood brought on by his last, astonishing dream was ebbing from him. It was as though the old Bensons, even Ebenezer, even Jamie, were the characters in a book once read during a feverish illness.

His soft feet plodded across the bridges, crunching dangerously on the broken glass. Soon he was at the open arch where Jamie's inscription seemed fresh and clear in the slanting sunlight.

When, in the dream, he had walked back from that place of fire and shadow, how *far* . . . ?

Slowly, with no thought now for a watching enemy, he paced the distance to the Cave. At the inset door he reached for his pocket-knife – then saw that the screws of the padlock hasp were gone! He stared stupidly at the door, seeing that its edge was half an inch away from the jamb; yellow light flickered up and down the sliver of blackness. Involuntarily he grasped the edge and yanked the door open.

The sudden draught made the candle flame dance crazily, sending shadows darting and jumping against the packed shelves. Half a dozen faces stared in his direction. Lenny Eccles was slumped in Andy's car seat, the others stood or squatted round. They had raided one of the packing cases and helped themselves to the quaint, battered railwaymen's caps which they wore idiotically tilted on their heads. Tunics and other equipment lay scuffed in the dust of the floor.

Lenny Eccles started to drag himself from the low seat. 'Grab him!'

They came at Phil in a bunch, and Phil backed out of the doorway and ran. He did not think of bravery, or cowardice. He merely felt sickened and bewildered because the last of his secrets had been wrenched from him. Something evil and alien had polluted his Cave, and it was no longer his. But something else *was*, in a way, and confusedly he knew he must get these oafish, meddlesome boys away from it.

He got clear of the embankment, the V of the twin railway branches. He raced for a few wild yards along the viaduct path, then turned and clawed through the rusty wire fence bounding the waste ground. He felt his clothes rip against the barbs, the trickle of blood on his legs and arms as he dragged himself free. Hardly noticing the stings, he dashed thirty yards across the rough turf towards the huddle of abandoned car wrecks.

He gained the shelter of the first, letting himself go, slithering on his stomach under the rust-eaten old chassis. He lay there, panting, pivoting round so that he could mark the way he had come from the viaduct.

At first he could see no one. A train rattled by and the ground trembled beneath him. The coarse grass and weeds pricked his face and hands. He began easing himself forward, wriggling on his elbows, trying to improve his vantage point, and then, between the rotting tyres of the front wheels, he saw them. Two, three, four boys spread out wide across the Wasteland, wearing their railway caps, advancing slowly towards the old car. They walked without stealth, knowing where Phil was, several times bending down on their way to pick up things from the ground.

Something heavy and metallic struck the bonnet of the car, bounced off and hid itself in the grass. A second object whistled overhead. A voice drawled, 'Come out, Benson, we've got you!'

Phil got up, breaking cover then, running a gauntlet of hissing, clanging 'missiles', headed for the tangle of buildings at the end of the path, the way he had come after leaving Andy. Andy would be back there, somewhere, perhaps near the shops, unless he had simply gone back home in disgust.

But Phil did not get far. He realized, now, that Lenny Eccles and another of the bigger boys had run ahead, and at a tangent from the others. Now they were waiting, their capped heads just visible behind a rubbish heap. Phil turned again and sprinted between the two groups back towards the fence, momentarily taking the gang by surprise. At this point the fence was tall, a six foot obstacle of chain wire supported by steel posts. He used his fingers and toes to climb up and over it, knowing that the heavier boys, wearing leather shoes, would have more trouble getting across.

Phil dropped on the other side, his feet stinging through the soles of his plimsolls. The Eccles gang had stopped throwing things, now, too occupied with trying to find a quick way through the fence, darting to and fro beyond the wire mesh like caged animals.

They would have to go along some way to come through

the barbed wire section, and Phil had a start on them. He used it, running lightly, but with pounding heart, tracking back along beside the viaduct in the opposite direction. When he was sure that no feet were thudding in pursuit, he slipped through an open arch into a yard used by a firm of transport trucks, a place deserted on Sundays. Certain, now, that he had temporarily shaken the gang off he twisted and climbed over broken walls and rubbish mounds until he found a clear course on the other side of the railway.

Here were the backs of the arch stores and workshops, and few were accessible from this side. Most, like the Cave, were bricked in at the other ends. But Phil remembered that, just where some huge council flats loomed on the edge of Deptford centre, a brief trespass over a garden wall would bring him to a narrow alley leading straight to the rear of a garage situated in the arches. And the garage *was* open on Sundays. Phil climbed the wall, slipped past the viaduct path again, with Eccles's Yard a few yards away.

'Phil!' Andy and Molly had reached the secret passage into the 'jungle'. They had been arguing for some time whether to make an immediate attempt to rescue Phil, or enlist Mr Felix's help first. Phil's sudden appearance from the garage was a relief. 'Crumbs, you look as if you've been run over by a train!'

Phil shook his head. His clothes were filthy and torn, and there were grazes and scratches all over his hands and face. 'I'm okay. The Cave is blown, did you know?'

Andy nodded. Molly explained as they picked their way through the jungle. She was still talking when they reached the barbed wire boundary. Then she stopped.

Sitting on her upturned piano was Lenny Eccles. Several of his gang had propped themselves against the swing posts and the walls of the shed. 'There's a short cut to this place,' sneered Lenny, 'Remind me to show it to you some time!'

The boys slowly formed a wide circle round them. Lenny Eccles picked up a thick length of wood that was lying there. It had once formed part of the garden fence, and, feet astride, he began swinging it like a fat golf club. 'We'll talk nice and quiet. We don't want to waken that old geezer in the house, do we? Now, which of you lot is going to tell us where the stuff is. The stuff you took from that arch?'

'It's where *you* can't get it,' said Andy, and his eyes turned towards the house at the bottom of the garden.

Lenny did not look surprised. 'So the old man *is* sticking his nose in, is he? I know somebody who's going to be interested to hear that.' His half stupid, half cunning stare rested on Phil for a moment; then, tauntingly, it switched to Molly Perkins. 'Of course, you might be having us on ... you might not have taken whatever-it-is to the old man at all. You could have hidden it up here somewhere. In the shed? No, we've taken a butcher's there. Under that pile of muck? Too wet.' Now his eyes dropped to the old piano. 'I bet there's room in that for a few old pieces-of-eight, or a map to Treasure Island, or gold nuggets ...?'

The Eccles boy looked round at his grinning gang. Suddenly he gave a tug at the railwayman's cap, lifted the heavy post above his head and swung it down on the naked piano strings. There was a frightening discord, and the old instrument's side panel split open from its damp joints. The single blow had been enough to destroy it, but Lenny smashed the post down again and again, his face grimacing with malicious delight, until little bits of wood and metal flew all round the garden. To the last, the piano moaned hollowly as though it were a live thing.

Molly Perkins watched the destruction with tight lips. Then, when it was over at last, she sat back on a mound of rubbish and cried. She cried aloud and broken heartedly, trying to catch the big tears with the grubby sleeve of her cardigan. Phil and Andy stood by, helpless. The girl's reaction to Lenny's mean, spiteful act shocked and embarrassed them.

Lenny giggled. The others began to mimic Molly's unashamed sobbing, mimed the heave of her shoulders and the way she buried her face in her hands. Then, with a burst of fury that took everybody by surprise, she reached for the post that Lenny had slung down. Her sobs turned into curses. She swung the post in a deadly arc, catching Lenny Eccles smack across the shoulders. The big boy gave a curious gulp, staggered, then stumbled towards the fence with his hands spread out defensively like a scarecrow's.

His gang backed away, their eyes wide with fright and astonishment. The terrible post whirled round and round. As Molly pursued them remorsely into the jungle her progress was that of a crazed tigress. Andy and Phil, laughing now, heard the crackle as the thin branches of the stunted trees snapped with the force of the swinging post. Yells and screams gradually faded beyond the jungle, out there on the viaduct path. . . .

Then Phil and Andy were suddenly aware that Mr Felix had joined them at the trellis. He was looking sadly at the smashed piano. 'Now that was a pity,' he said, tut-tutting. 'That was a rotten thing for those vandals to do. That girl really does have a remarkable ear for music.'

'There – you'll live,' said Mr Felix, fixing the last of four strips of sticking plaster on Phil's damaged limbs. 'Let's go into the other room, I've rather a lot to tell you.'

'About the surprise you mentioned?' asked Andy.

The enthusiast smiled secretively. 'Not so fast, my lad. I suppose you've had your breakfast?'

Phil suddenly remembered that he hadn't. Mr Felix wanted to cook him eggs and bacon, but Phil shook his head. After the excitement of the chase, the exhilaration of Molly's counter-attack on the Eccles gang, his pale, haunted, Benson look had returned.

He sat uninterestedly stirring a plate of cereal while Mr Felix, evidently with some orderly purpose in mind, assembled Documents X in neat array on the table. 'Now, where to begin? The diaries, I think. Poor Ebenezer may have had his odd ways and, as we all know, his handwriting was atrocious. But it would be wrong to think of him as mad. These diaries give a very lucid account of everything he felt from the day he moved into Landmann Street until a short time before his early and tragic death.' Mr Felix looked up at the sunlit window, his face serious, the pose of a genial eccentric gone. 'Here we have an engineering genius of perhaps the first rank. The diaries tell little of what went wrong in Newcastle – why there was that quarrel with George Stephenson, for instance. Stephenson was a great and generous character, but he had strong ideas of his own about what was practicable and what was not ... perhaps, in the early stages, Ebenezer's *Stormrider* was too *much* of a dream. And Ebenezer was stubborn, sensitive and he would not have reacted with patience to the official pig-headedness that, I'm afraid, thwarted so many original minds at the beginning of the Railway Age. ...' The enthusiast smiled faintly at his cat, washing its whiskers on the sideboard. 'Your ancestor, young Benson, seems, in some ways, to have resembled another great but disappointed pioneer – Richard Trevithick. Did you know, by the way, that he, too, is buried not so far away – in Dartford?'

Phil nodded. Mr Felix went on, 'But Ebenezer had more determination. When he came south he was set on building his engine, somehow, somewhere, with or without official encouragement. He went on working at his plans, day and night, for over a year. He believed desperately in the *Stormrider* – his "Child of Brass and Iron" as he called it. It was something new, something that would change the history of the railways, and at first he wanted to bring it to birth at the forge more than anything else in the world. . . .'

'At first?' whispered Phil.

Mr Felix looked at him. 'Yes . . . we'll come to that in a minute. Now, when I first studied the plans, and read the earlier part of the diaries, I asked myself some questions. I sat here and did a little dreaming myself. Suppose, I thought, Ebenezer *had* built the *Stormrider*. How would he go about it?' Mr Felix lifted the old accounts book from the table and opened it on his knee. 'Well, he had the money . . . more than enough, even after he had built his house.'

'The money he hid away, because he was a miser!' cried Andy.

Mr Felix's lips twisted. 'He had the money. What else would he need? First, a place to build it, but that would be very difficult because he wanted to carry out the work in secret. The diaries tell us that he was in dread lest his ideas be stolen, or copied, by others with a better chance than he had for obtaining official encouragement. Then he would have to have some of the work carried out at specialist forges and factories, and shipped to the point of assembly. If, for instance, he'd set up his workshop here in Deptford, some parts would have to be brought by sea from the north, then along the Thames and the canal. He would need labour, of course . . . and engineers of skill, men he could trust not to reveal his secret until the day arrived for the *Stormrider* to be brought out on tracks and shown to the world – or, more particularly perhaps, the London and Greenwich Railway. If the North wouldn't have Ebenezer's "child", perhaps the South would, when they saw its wonders with their own eyes. . . .' The enthusiast gave himself a little smile. 'Yes, I dreamed quite a lot. In the midst of reading the diary for eighteen-forty-three I asked myself, "Well, why not? Why didn't it all come to be?" '

'He died too soon,' said Andy.

'Yes . . . in a way. But somebody else died first – the young fellow in the daguerreotype, Jamie. . . .' Phil stirred and Mr Felix reached for one of the diaries. 'I thought I had the answer, why Ebenezer never built the *Stormrider*, when I came across this entry. I'll read it to you: "There can be no forgiveness on earth or in Heaven, if my Child of Brass and Iron should live, and dear Jamie die. . . ." There is more in similar vein. You see, Ebenezer felt a great sense of guilt, because his son had become sick. He needed medical care, so many things Ebenezer was denying him. . . .'

'Because he was *saving up* to build the loco?' Again it was Andy who asked the questions, with Phil wooden and brooding beside him. 'And he felt that, instead of hoarding that money and half starving his family, he ought. . . .'

'He ought to give up the idea of building his "Child of Brass and Iron", and think of his flesh and blood children, especially Jamie? Yes . . . but by then it was too late. Nearly all the money was gone. . . .'

'But *how*?'

Mr Felix pointed to the cash book. 'It's all there, only it took me a while to see it from the right point of view. Those amounts of money that you and Phil's grandfather, apparently, thought were hoardings were nothing of the kind. They were *spendings*. You see, what none of the old Bensons could ever have known, or told if they had, was that Ebenezer *did* build the *Stormrider*. A few months after that tragic entry in the diary, the locomotive was almost complete and young Jamie was dead. The money was spent, and Ebenezer told himself that Jamie had paid the price of his ambition and fanatical obstinacy. . .'

Andy gasped. 'Then . . . what happened to the *Stormrider*?'

'The last pages of the diary for eighteen-forty-four make that quite clear. Ebenezer swore his labourers to secrecy and had his secret workshop sealed, bricked in. He punished himself by burying his child of iron, he thought, for ever. . . .'

'Where – *where*?'

And it was Phil who answered. 'In the viaduct, under the workshops where he was manager. It never was gold, Andy. It's the *Stormrider*, and it's still there!'

16 'Child of Brass and Iron'

Mr Felix gathered Documents X together. 'So much to do . . . so many people to consult. The Ministry of Transport, British Rail – perhaps various preservation societies. The diaries don't pinpoint the exact location, but there must be old records in existence as to where the workshops were. Who knows what we shall find, once the ball is set rolling?'

Andy chuckled. 'I hope the place is bang next to old Eccles's junk yard. He's got a lot of stuff stored in some of the arches, too. I can't wait to see his face when the bulldozers turn up!'

Mr Felix looked shocked. 'Hardly bulldozers, my lad. They'll have to use more subtle means.' He glanced out of the window up his stretch of unkempt garden. 'I'm almost tempted to go out there now, pick and spade and all . . . but no, that would be a trifle precipitate. It'll be an experts' affair now and, I'm afraid, you boys will have to bow out as gracefully as you can. Not that there won't be a great deal going on to interest you . . . oh, and I must have a talk with your uncle, young man.'

'It'll be a big disappointment for him,' smiled Phil.

Mr Felix yawned. 'Yes, but you never know. He *is* a Benson, and I dare say he is capable of feeling family pride of the right sort. And of course, there will be some money involved. . . .'

At Landmann Street there was the story to tell, Phil's sticking plasters to explain, and then Aunt Luce let fly at Uncle Ern rather like a grown-up version of Molly Perkins.

'There! What have I been telling you, all along? All that rubbish about a nest-egg.'

153

'How was I to know?' blustered Uncle Ern. 'The old man and his yarns ever since I was so-high ... and then that lodger O'Reilly ...'

Aunt Luce said just what she thought of Mr O'Reilly, and went on, 'And pestering the life out of Phil. ...'

'Well, he shouldn't've winkled out them papers without permission.'

'He *had* permission – from his grandad. And getting that Eccles lot to half murder him. ...'

'Oh, come off it! What's a couple of scratches? And if it'll make you any happier I'll go straight over there and belt that Lenny Eccles. ...'

'It's his father you ought to belt. He didn't do you any good when you were in business years ago, and you shouldn't have taken up with him now.'

'I didn't take up with him. I just happened to run across him in the pub. ...' Uncle Ern looked sheepishly at Phil. His bitterness and enmity seemed spent. 'Who's this Felix character, and where does he fit in?'

Phil told him, adding. 'He thinks the stuff's worth quite a lot of money. ...'

Uncle Ern's pale eyes took on an odd expression. He fingered his ear for a moment, breathing heavily. Then he said, 'What d'you think I am? A blinking grave robber? Money's money and a man's entitled to his rights. But that sort of junk, well – it's *history*, isn't it?'

Events took place with dreadful slowness. What Uncle Ern referred to as 'wagonloads of red tape' had, apparently, to be unwound, then wound up again. Then they turned out to be the wrong sort of tape, or the wrong people did the winding.

Maps and diagrams were sought, found, lost, recovered again in mistaken pigeonholes in obscure office buildings. At last came the measurers, surveyors and railway historians. 'All we want now are the court magicians!' commented Uncle Ern.

They found the site. Then they said that they thought they had found what *might* be the site. At last they were sure. It was definitely not Phil's Cave nor, to Andy's chagrin, was it anywhere near Eccles's junk yard. It was almost certainly, they said, below a brewery, but they would have to break through from next door, in an arch used for the storage of chemicals.

The chemical firm said that nobody was going to disturb their chemicals: anything could happen if they tried, there might be explosions. Surely, it was patiently pointed out, experts from the chemical firm could remove the containers safely? Yes, said the chemical firm, but they were too busy. Exports were more important than history. But, the argument went on, if the chemicals were due to be exported, wouldn't they be moved soon anyway? There was talk of something called injunctions, court proceedings and the liberty of the individual to store his chemicals where he chose.

Suddenly, for no known reason, the chemical firm gave in. The specialists made their plans, and one sunny summer morning the excavating party began work. Throughout all these negotiations and discussions Mr Felix had remained serene. Now the hour had arrived, his temper was uncertain. He was 'short' with a local newspaperman who wanted to interview him. He was shorter still with Uncle Ern who said, 'Why don't you just borrow a pneumatic drill and bust through? All this picking and tapping's going to get us nowhere.'

'Really, Mr Benson, surely you know better than that! They're going to enter a chamber which has been sealed – practically airtight – for a century and a quarter. You'll be suggesting the use of dynamite next!'

The morose way in which Uncle Ern rolled his fifteenth

cigarette of the morning implied that in his opinion this wouldn't be a bad idea.

By afternoon they had scraped away the brickwork of the inner, communicating arch and, reeling back in disgust from the waves of foul, gassy air that assailed them, exposed the crumbled steps descending into blackness.

Phil, who with Andy was to accompany the excavators, realized, without particular disappointment, that the dream had been wrong about these, too. They were not spiral steps. They just dropped steep and straight into the abyss.

The leading men wore overalls, protective masks and miners' lamps fixed to steel helmets. They went on alone, their feet crunching on the old steps. There was a brief silence, then the pioneers crunched back again, masks removed, giving the thumbs-up sign. Mr Felix, the boys, Uncle Ern and various other privileged guests donned their borrowed helmets and followed the leaders down.

They all gathered, like visitors to an Egyptian tomb, at the foot of the stairs. The excavators used powerful hand torches to light the scene. The cavern was not so large as had been expected, just large enough. Anonymous pieces of equipment leaned against the walls, like soldiers at a lying-in-state, grown thin and fallen asleep.

In the middle, on tracks, stood the locomotive. The beams of the torches threw back no reflections from the long entombed monster, for she was encrusted with grime and corrosion.

But one of the engineers stepped closer. 'A bit of spit and polish'll make all the difference,' he said. He rubbed carefully at her side with a piece of rag. Gradually, one by one, the letters on the chassis took form out of the darkness:

STORMRIDER

' "Child of Brass and Iron",' quoted Mr Felix, softly.

'She looks . . . complete,' whispered Andy.

'But she isn't, quite,' said Phil. 'Jamie died, and Ebenezer blamed himself and the *Stormrider*, so he had her bricked in, and there she has lain, and nobody knew.'

The enthusiast nodded. 'Only a handful of carefully picked labourers and technicians – men who wouldn't talk, or who were soon going abroad, others who were deaf and dumb. But it was a remarkable achievement, to have reserved this part of the old engine repair depot for his own purposes, smuggling gigantic sections on secret orders along the river. He must have been quite a character.'

Andy was perplexed. 'But – was it all *necessary*?'

'Who can say what was necessary to a genius like Ebenezer Benson? He felt cheated, forgotten, despised and misunderstood. He wanted to *show* them. His glorious day was to have been the day they took her out on the viaduct, hauling her up there on chains – a new *Rocket*, a second *Rainhill Trial* . . . but it was not to be.'

'He must, in a way, have loved *Stormrider*,' murmured Phil.

'Yes, but he loved Jamie the more. A man like Ebenezer loves passionately. He was a man of two loves, and we know what happened when one object of that love seemed, in poor Ebenezer's twisted mind, to have killed the other. It was the end.'

'No,' said Phil. 'No, not now. Not the *end*.'

The party ahead of them stirred. A man coughed in the lingering stench of the cavern. Others began talking of the practical concerns which lay ahead. For them, the *Stormrider* was an episode, a relic of interest, a passing challenge to their antiquarian wits.

For Phil she was a heritage.

Several years went by – years of growing and learning and sharing. One day, at Waterloo Station, a young man leaned his elbows on the open window frame of a railway carriage. He wore, at a jaunty tilt, the white-crowned peaked cap of a Radio Officer in the Merchant Marine Service. Everything about him was fresh, new and confident. This was to be his first long voyage, from Southampton to Rio de Janeiro.

A second young man was seeing him off. He stood uneasily on the platform, a slimmer, more carelessly dressed figure. His dark eyes and sallow expression gave him that far-away, other-worldly look, which could be rather deceiving. When roused, he could be as alert and practical as most. It was merely, said people, the Benson look.

A whistle shrilled. 'Well, this is it,' said Andy.

'I don't think so. It's the other platform,' said Phil.

'Oh!' Andy had not yet developed the sailor's casualness at parting.

'You will write?'

'Of course! Maybe only a postcard at first. You know how it is.'

Phil grinned. 'Bet you'll manage more than that for Molly!'

Andy laughed noncommittally. 'Madame Beethoven!' His mind searched for words to fill the last moments. 'Remember the day she thumped that Lenny Eccles?'

They both laughed at the remembering.

Andy went on, pretending seriousness. 'Hey, I've just thought ... isn't your technical college near that music school she goes to?'

'I don't know. Anyway, I don't start till next month. If it is, I'll keep an eye on her for you!'

Andy wagged a warning finger. 'It had better be no more than that, brother!' Then he said, serious again. 'Pretty decent of old Felix, wasn't it? Paying for those piano lessons and all that ... remember the old piano? Cripes, that row – like playing a concerto on an outsized jew's-harp! Funny, though, that it turned out she did have a bit of talent after all. . . .'

The right whistle blew. Awkwardly, Andy stuck out a hand and grasped Phil's. 'Rio, here we come! Give the *Stormrider* a pat for me when you see her. Lucky devil! When you're at college you'll be able to call in at the museum every day if you want. . . .'

The train crept away. Phil walked along, keeping pace. Phil said, 'I'll miss you around, Andy.'

Andy clipped him playfully on the chin. 'You've been okay, too, for a dreaming Benson . . . by the way, did you ever keep that queer penny?'

The train drew off, faster. Phil made no reply. It was so odd that Andy had asked that question. During all the years, he had never once mentioned the penny – not after that single, hopeless effort to explain.

Andy waved. Phil waved.

When the train had dwindled, Phil swung quickly away for the ticket barrier.

On the other side he stopped, oblivious of the bustle around him. He took the thin, black coin from the small zipped pocket which was one of its hiding places. He let it lie on his palm for a second and as he looked at it his adam's apple slowly rose and fell.

Then he gave it a single, careful toss and returned it to his pocket. He went off whistling towards his bus, trying to think of other things. What would Aunt Luce have ready for his tea? Would Uncle Ern spend the evening with his cronies or stay at home and watch TV?

But Andy's question came back, and back. Perhaps, after all, he had tried to understand. And if not, Phil had been wrong to let bitterness rise between them.

You shared adventures; presently, even secrets were open books; together you were the treasure seekers.

But you dreamed alone.